"A lot of things about your life have taken me by surprise."

"I feel the same way about seeing you, LizBeth." Jackson paused, then added, "It's a good thing, though. I always wondered how you were."

"Really?"

"I knew when I left that I would probably be shunned. That kept me from asking too much, but I did think about everyone and wonder how they were doing. Especially you."

Especially her. Feeling like her mouth had just gone dry, LizBeth murmured, "Is that right?"

"Of course I thought you would have gotten married by now. I never imagined that you would've left the church, too. I wish I had known that."

"Even if we could no longer have been together, we could have still kept in touch, Jackson. At the very least, you could've written me a letter after you left." Unable to help herself, she added, "Or any other time during the last twelve years."

Shelley Shepard Gray writes inspirational and sweet contemporary romances for a variety of publishers. With over a million books in print, and translated into more than a dozen languages, her novels have reached both the *New York Times* and the *USA TODAY* bestseller lists. Shelley's novels have also been featured in a variety of national publications.

In addition to her writing, Shelley has hosted several well-attended Girlfriend Getaways for Amish reading fans. Her most recent Girlfriend Getaway, hosted with several other novelists, was highlighted on Netflix's *Follow This* series.

Before writing romances, Shelley taught school and earned her bachelor's degree in English literature and later obtained her master's degree in educational administration. She now lives in southern Colorado near her grown children, walks her dachshunds, bakes too much and writes full-time.

Also by Shelley Shepard Gray

Inspirational Cold Case Collection

Widow's Secrets

AMISH JANE DOE

SHELLEY SHEPARD GRAY

LOVE INSPIRED

INSPIRATIONAL ROMANCE

LOVE INSPIRED®
INSPIRATIONAL ROMANCE

Recycling programs for this product may not exist in your area.

ISBN-13: 978-1-335-42609-3

Amish Jane Doe

Copyright © 2022 by Shelley Sabga

For questions and comments about the quality of this book, please contact us at CustomerService@Harlequin.com.

Love Inspired
22 Adelaide St. West, 41st Floor
Toronto, Ontario M5H 4E3, Canada
www.LoveInspired.com

Printed in U.S.A.

Though I walk through the valley of the shadow of death, I will fear no evil: for thou art with me.
—*Psalm* 23:4

What you do is more revealing than anything you might say.
—Amish Proverb

For all the readers who wanted to know
what happened to Mose Kramer, the sheriff
in my Crittenden County books. I hope you'll be
as pleased as I was to see him again.

Acknowledgments

I'm so grateful to my editor, Johanna Raisanen,
for the opportunity to write this book. Johanna
not only gave me the green light to write the book
I wanted to write, she also was so encouraging and
helpful. I often say that I'm the type of writer who
needs an editor, and she really is one of the best.

I'm also indebted to the entire team at Harlequin
for the awesome cover, the careful copy editing,
and the amazing marketing and promotion
for these Cold Case novels.
I love being a part of this team!

I also owe a big thanks to Lynne Stroup,
who read and edited this novel in just a week so
I could turn it in on time, to my Buggy Bunch FB
group and to my husband, Tom, for helping me
come up with this novel's plot. Finally, I'm indebted
to my readers, who have stayed with me
all these years. I couldn't be more grateful.

Chapter One

Busy's Amish Market still smelled the same, like fresh bread, strawberries, lemon furniture polish and clean cotton. Added to the mix had always been the faint tart scent of spicy mustard. Jackson Lapp had never understood the last element, but LizBeth Troyer had never revealed what it was. All she'd ever done when he had asked was smile and say it was a family secret.

He'd thought that answer had been adorable. No, back when they were teenagers, he'd considered practically everything his girlfriend had done adorable.

He hadn't thought much about Busy's, the store's scents or even LizBeth during the past twelve years. Though he'd been through a lot, that hadn't been the reason. No, it had a whole lot more to do with his heart than his busy life. It was far too tempting to try to forget his former life instead of dwelling on the things he couldn't have anymore. Even after all this time, it was still painful to remember how smitten he'd once been with both LizBeth and their quiet, quaint Plain life.

Those sweet, innocent days seemed so long ago.

As he walked farther into the crowded and cluttered store located on the outskirts of Berlin, Ohio, Jackson tried to get his bearings. No, that wasn't exactly true. He was actually coming up with a number of reasons it would be best for everyone—most especially himself—if he simply walked right back out the door.

There were a great number of reasons that he should leave, and not just personal ones, either. Professional ones as well, since he was a cop in Cincinnati, not Berlin. He didn't have any pull here, and it was obvious that he no longer even fit in. It was doubtful many of the Amish in the community would recognize him. Or if they did, they might not trust him.

Which made it even more surprising that he'd worked hard to persuade his lieutenant to give him two days to gather information on their Jane Doe.

Every time he thought about the way the girl had been found, in the back room of a seedy hotel with needle marks in her arm, he'd felt sick to his stomach. Seeing the discarded *kapp* neatly folded in the tote under that cot had nearly taken his breath away. The girl, obviously still a teenager, had been Amish.

There were a lot of Amish living in the state of Ohio, though. Added to the fact that most Amish didn't have social security numbers or school records and lived a relatively isolated existence, the poor girl's identity had never been discovered.

It was only when he'd taken a closer look at one of the crime scene photographs that he'd felt a ray of hope. That *kapp* had been found in a signature tote from Busy's Market. Of course, the victim having such a tote bag might not mean a thing.

But it might.

There were also several other roadblocks to overcome. Busy Troyer, the owner of the Amish market, had long since gone to the Lord. He wasn't even sure who ran the market now, but there was a very good chance whoever it was would be reluctant to help him at all. Not too many Amish wanted much to do with an *Englischer* cop from Cincinnati.

But he still had to try.

Glad that the woman behind the counter was busy helping customers, Jackson kept to the outside aisles of the store. Between the crowd in the shop and the slightly dark room—on account of there being no electricity—he was able to blend in and further weigh the pros and cons.

No, he was able to at last face the main reason why he didn't want to stay in the building. It held far too many memories—both good and bad. This store, this treasure trove of goodies and junk, held some of the best moments in his life. He'd first tried candy bars here. And eaten too many apple cider donuts.

He'd watched the *Englisch* and wondered about them, while holding his baby sister's hand.

But most of all, the only memories that actually mattered were the ones that had to do with the pretty girl who seemed to always be at the store. He'd first met LizBeth in this very space when he was seven. They'd become fast friends when they'd been nine. They'd annoyed each other to no end when they were thirteen…and he'd fallen in love with LizBeth when he was sixteen.

He'd even tried to kiss her once in the very aisle he was standing in.

Looking at all the pots, pans and serving spoons,

Jackson blinked. Why had he even wandered over in that direction?

"Can I help you?"

He started, then gaped as he found the owner of the sweet, melodic voice. "LizBeth," he said before he could remind himself to keep quiet.

A haunted look appeared on her face. No doubt, it was a match to his own expression. Ignoring the five or so people who'd just walked to the counter, she stepped toward him.

Jackson couldn't help himself from cataloging her appearance. She still had the same dark hair that was straight and shone like a mink's coat. Still had the same matching dark brown eyes framed by dark eyelashes. She still had the same faint scar near her upper lip from when she'd fallen on a rock and bit clear through it. She'd cried and carried on so much, her parents didn't make her go to the doctor to get a good set of stitches. Instead, he'd held her hand while her *daed* patched her up.

She was still perfect and beautiful and had a way of looking at him that made him want to be better inside. Where it counted.

The only thing that differed was that years ago, before he'd left the area in the middle of the night, the last time he'd seen her, she'd been wearing a *kapp*, black stockings and a light gray dress fastened together with straight pins.

Now she had on jeans, a long-sleeved T-shirt and designer tennis shoes. And, of course, her hair was now hanging down her shoulders instead of being modestly pinned up under a prayer covering.

It seemed he wasn't the only person in their small community who was no longer Amish.

Staring at Jackson Lapp, the man she'd once loved and who'd left her without a word following one of the most embarrassing and horrible nights of her life, LizBeth Troyer didn't know whether to hug him, ask him a dozen questions or slap his cheek. Because he looked far too confident after all the pain and trauma he'd put her through.

"What are you doing here?"

He waited a few seconds before answering. "I'm here because of a case I'm working on."

Needles of disappointment pinched her heart as she processed his reply. "A case?"

"I'm a police officer now." When still she gaped, he added, "You know, a cop."

"I know what a police officer is, Jackson. If I'm looking shocked, it's because I thought you were dead."

"What?"

She was slightly pleased to see that now he was the one staring in confusion. "No one spoke your name," she added. "Your parents acted as if you'd never existed. And your little sister? Well, she just looked haunted."

"I hate to hear that." Marie had been only six when he'd left.

Seeing the same hurt look in his eyes that she was feeling in her heart, LizBeth felt her insides shift a bit. Maybe she didn't exactly hate him any longer. But she sure did want some answers.

"LizBeth!" Harlan called out. "I need ya."

Harlan was a second cousin. He was helpful and

hardworking but young, which meant that she couldn't ignore his summons. "I've got to go."

Jackson craned his neck. "Who's that?"

She couldn't believe he was acting like she was going to give him information just because he asked. "That is none of your business."

"Look, I know you probably have a dozen questions for me, but I really need to talk to you."

"Now isn't the time. I'm really busy, you know."

To his credit, Jackson didn't comment on the half-empty store. "When might you be free?"

"I don't know." She ran a hand through her hair, pushing back the thick locks that she'd mistakenly thought would be a nice change to have hanging down her back instead of neatly tied up like she usually wore them.

"Look, I'm staying in Millersburg. Is there a pizza place or something still around there?"

"There is. The Garden Goat."

"How about we meet there at six? I'll buy you supper."

"That isn't necessary."

Ignoring her comment, he looked at the front door. "Do you still close at sundown?"

"We do."

"So will you meet me? It's important, LizBeth."

She gaped at him, hating that she remembered how he used to beg her to sneak out to meet him because seeing each other only once a day wasn't near often enough. Every time, he would whisper in her ear that seeing her was important to him.

"Please?" Jackson prodded.

Harlan's sixteen-year-old voice squeaked. "LizBeth, I really need ya!"

"Hold on, I'll be right there!" she called out before turning back to Jackson. "I'm sorry, but I really do have to go."

"Will I see you at six?"

"Jah."

"Danke."

Their brief whispered exchange in Pennsylvania Dutch brought a smile to her face before she hurried to the counter.

"May I help you?" she asked the woman in line.

"These things, please."

Realizing that her cousin had simply gotten overwhelmed because there were three customers in line, LizBeth started ringing up the woman's purchases.

Looking more at ease, Harlan leaned closer. "Who was that *Englisch* guy you were talking to?"

"No one. Just a guy I used to know."

"Who?"

"Not now, Harlan," she murmured in a low tone before smiling at the woman. "I'm so glad you visited Busy's today. Did you find everything you were looking for?"

LizBeth had no idea what the woman said in return, but it didn't matter. All that did was that she was going to see Jackson Lapp again in just a few hours.

She hoped he'd never realize how excited she was about that.

Chapter Two

Jackson had no reason to stick around Busy's, but he couldn't think of anything he'd rather do than watch LizBeth for a few more minutes. She'd flitted through the area, chatting with a new customer, murmuring encouragement to her cousin, straightening a crooked line of jars on one of the shelves.

He found every little thing she did fascinating.

For almost a dozen years, he'd tortured himself with regrets and second guesses about how he left LizBeth without a word and how he could've handled things during their last night together. No, how he *should* have handled things their last night together. No matter how dysfunctional his family had been, he'd known better than to treat LizBeth the way he had.

It was no wonder he'd spent hours hating himself for the way he'd behaved when she'd been in his arms... and the hours following.

Thinking back, flashes of the evening hit him hard. The party at Emersons' barn. The feeling of reckless-ness he'd had, combined with the deep-seated need to feel something—anything good. He hadn't been the only Amish teen who'd felt that way. Most of the kids gathering in the barn had been eager to try all kinds of taboo activities. Some were as simple and sweet as watching movies on hidden DVD players.

Other kids, of course, had been eager to dabble in drinking and smoking. Others were driving cars without licenses to fast-food restaurants. Or any place where their parents wouldn't see them.

Where they could pretend—just for a little while— that their futures weren't already set.

LizBeth had been far more circumspect. Rebellion for her had been an occasional touch of lipstick and going to the mall with a few *Englisch* friends.

He, on the other hand, had felt almost a frenzied need to try anything he could.

That had been a direct result of his home life, of course. His father was cruel and often looked for reasons to punish him. His mother, worn down by living with such a man, had become adept at pretending to not be aware of what was happening to Jackson.

And, living as they did on their isolated farm, Jackson had always known that anything could happen and no one from the outside world would ever know what had occurred.

But that last night had been so very bad. He'd done things he shouldn't. Worse, he'd encouraged LizBeth to do them, too. The other kids had egged them on.

Or at least that was what he'd told himself.

Then, right past midnight, LizBeth's brother Frank had ventured in, discovered the two of them kissing passionately. Within seconds, he'd yelled at them both and practically marched them into his buggy. It had been humiliating.

While LizBeth had been trying hard not to get sick in the car, Frank yelled at Jackson the whole way to his house. Feeling like he deserved every word LizBeth's brother said, Jackson had sat quietly and listened.

But then everything had gotten a whole lot worse after Frank deposited him on his doorstep.

Jackson's father had been waiting for him. After hearing only a few seconds of Jackson's story, he got out a belt and beat him mercilessly. Then he made Jackson spend the night in a stall in the barn. His parting words had been that more would happen in the morning.

Some parents might say such things but wouldn't mean them. They'd be empty threats uttered in the heat of the moment.

However, Jackson had known that his father meant every word.

And so late that night, he broke the barn's door, crept into the house, grabbed what few possessions he'd had, including the hundred dollars in cash that he'd secretly collected over the last two years, and left without a single word or even a note.

He'd never regretted leaving.

But he did regret how he'd never sent even a letter to LizBeth, trying to explain why he'd left.

As if she could read his mind, LizBeth looked up from the counter, seemed to scan the area for him and then almost smiled.

He smiled back before turning away. But just as he was striding toward the exit, the door opened again… and in walked his mother and Marie.

He practically ran into them. "Sorry," he said. "I

mean, hello, *Mamm*." He swallowed hard, barely able to take his eyes off his sister. "Hiya, Marie."

Both women stopped and gaped at him, just as if they were seeing a ghost. And maybe they were. He certainly did feel like a shadow of his former self. While the strained silence continued, he studied them both. His mother looked like she'd aged twenty or thirty years instead of twelve.

And Marie? Well, his sweet, darling little sister was no longer a curious, shy six-year-old but a beautiful eighteen-year-old young woman. He couldn't stop staring at her.

Her dark blond hair, the exact shade as his, was neatly pulled back from her face and concealed under a white *kapp*. But the knot of hair was so thick, it was obvious that her hair was still as long and voluminous as it had been when she was a young girl.

But it was her blue eyes which held him to her. They were as expressive as he'd remembered. The pain he spied in their depths almost took his breath away.

Anxious to find out what, exactly, had happened to her, Jackson stepped forward, eager to bridge the space. He was ready to say anything to get her to listen to him—even if just for a few brief moments. "Marie, *halt*," he murmured. "Let me talk to ya."

She almost leaned toward him. Her lips parted and she took a deep breath. She'd done the same thing when she was just a tiny thing. His sister would get so excited and anxious she'd have to steel herself in order to get the words out.

As if he'd never left, he leaned forward as well, silently letting her know that he'd wait as long as she needed for the words to come out.

"Marie, now," his mother said.

After the slightest pause, Marie straightened. Then, while he continued to stand in front of her, his sister turned and walked toward the back of the store. She didn't glance his way again. No, she acted as if he hadn't spoken a word.

That he wasn't still standing like a statue. As if he didn't matter. Didn't count.

Didn't exist.

Jackson knew for certain then that he'd been shunned. At least to his family. He was no longer anything to them.

Feeling as if he'd been struck anew, he felt his neck heat in embarrassment as they walked farther into the store.

Horrified by the rush of emotions coursing through him, Jackson walked through the door. Once outside, he took a deep breath and tried not to care that his little sister no longer could speak to him.

It shouldn't matter, anyway. After all, he was the one who'd made so many mistakes. He was the one who'd left without a word. This rift was all his fault, not hers.

Never hers.

Chapter Three

She was taking a terrible risk by attempting to speak to Jackson, but Marie had no choice. She was becoming desperate—and running out of time.

Of late, she'd been praying for the Lord to give her a sign to let her know that He'd been listening. Every morning, she'd remind the Lord about how unhappy she was, how dismal her future looked and how she was almost out of time.

For a full five minutes after she prayed, she would sit quietly on her neatly made bed and breathe deeply. Time and again, she'd feel His presence, almost hear His voice. And each time, she was sure He was encouraging her to believe. To not give up.

However, every time she got her hopes up, nothing happened. If anything, things had gotten worse. Each day, her world had felt more constrained and her outlook bleaker. Though her parents had become slightly more lenient after Jackson had left without a word in the middle of the night, they were a long way from acting like her friends' parents. So much so, she knew

that even if things did change a little, *Mamm* and *Daed*
would never be all that different.

Marta and Grace's parents liked to chat with them.
Play cards sometimes. Smiled. Marie's behaved far, far
differently. They expected things, too. Expected her to
work all the time. To always be modest, to always be
good. In short, to be everything they'd thought Jackson never was.

But, of course, he had been a good person—at least
to her. Though nearly eleven years separated them,
they'd been close when she was a little girl. He'd looked
after her when she'd trailed after him, and had tucked
her in bed when their mother had been too tired to do
so at the end of the day.

Jackson's absence had hurt, but she'd learned to survive on her own. It hadn't been easy, though—especially not after she graduated eighth grade and had
been forbidden to attend most of the gatherings the
other teenagers in the church district did.

However, when her mother had decided that reading
novels was a sin, Marie knew she had to do something.
They'd taken away her freedoms, her brother and even
her fictional escapes. It was too much.

Hurting, Marie had attempted to look at other ways
to escape the prison she was in. Although Aaron Zook's
offer to take her away still stood, she hadn't made up
her mind. So she'd even begun to consider eligible
men to marry. Surely, life with any man would be better than her situation at home. But just as she'd felt the
Lord's presence by her side, she also felt that He was
asking her to wait a little longer. But for what, she
didn't know.

Marie had almost given up ever finding a way out of

her house…but then Jackson had appeared. She knew it wasn't a coincidence. His unexpected appearance could only have come from the Lord's will.

But the clock was ticking.

Knowing that she would incur her mother's wrath, she murmured something about needing to use the restroom and darted out the door. Busy's Market had locked bathroom doors on the side of the building. Marie could only hope that her mother didn't notice she hadn't gotten the key from LizBeth before she left.

Pulse racing, Marie hurried down the steps leading off the store's front porch and walked to the parking lot. In the back area were two buggies. One of the horses was unhooked and nibbling on a nearby patch of grass. Their horse was still hooked up to the buggy and standing under the covering.

Closer to the door were three cars. One Marie had seen many times. She knew that had to be LizBeth's. Hurrying to the others, she looked in the windows and prayed with all her might.

And then it seemed that God had listened after all… because Jackson was still there.

He looked so different from the last time she'd seen him. He'd filled out and he looked so tough. Stalwart. Like he could handle any problem with ease and any bit of pain without flinching.

Hoping that was the case, she knocked on the driver's side door.

He looked startled but put his phone down. When he reached for the door handle, she shook her head and motioned for him to put his window down instead.

Jackson complied immediately. He reached for her hand, covering it with a feeling of security. "Marie, thank the good Lord. I didn't think you were going to acknowledge me."

His words were sweet. So sweet. But she couldn't allow herself to unbend enough to give in to the rush of emotion that even this small exchange was bringing. "I can't talk now. Can you meet me later?"

"Of course. Where and when?"

"Emersons' barn at half past ten?"

"Emersons' barn?" He whistled low. "That's still around?"

She didn't answer. Impatient, she pulled her hand out from under his. "Can you?"

Worry filled his eyes. "Marie, are you sure that's safe for you?"

"Yes or no, Jackson. Will you?"

"Yes. Of course."

Unable to help herself, she touched his bare forearm. "*Danke*," she said in a rush before hurrying to the side of the building where the bathrooms were.

By the grace of God, the women's restroom door was unlocked. She rushed inside and promptly locked it behind her.

Then she turned on the sink and splashed cold water on her face. The frigid dousing made her gasp, and water dripped down the front of her dress, chilling her neck and collarbone. But she took the uncomfortable feeling as yet another sign of His approval.

There was no reason the restroom should have been unlocked and empty, but it was. Whatever happened, she was grateful for His help. Perhaps He'd been listening to her prayers, after all.

The door handle jiggled. "Marie, are you in here?"

Her mother sounded anxious. Marie cleared her throat. "*Jah, Mamm.* I'll be right out."

"Are you all right?"

"Of course. I'm just washing my hands." Hurriedly, she turned on the sink. "Are you ready to leave?"

"*Nee.* I was concerned about you. That's all. I'll be in the shop."

"I'll be right there."

When Marie didn't hear another word, she breathed a sigh of relief. Her mother had left. Her subterfuge had worked.

Walking out of the bathroom, she almost ran into a mother with her young daughter. "Sorry."

"Do you have the key?" the woman asked.

"I'm sorry, I don't," she replied. "The door was open when I got here." She gave a small shrug before walking down the hall.

When she entered the main store again, Marie quickly located her mother near some medicines and home remedies. LizBeth was standing behind the counter, wrapping up an item in newspaper. She paused and glanced her way.

Marie stared back but didn't approach. Instead, she continued to her mother's side and picked up the wicker shopping basket that she'd placed on the ground. "Do you need me to get anything else for you, *Mamm*?"

After looking her over, her mother shrugged. "*Nee.* I'm almost finished. Give me a few more minutes and then we'll need to be on our way."

Marie nodded and stayed by her mother's side, hoping for all the world that she looked like any other obedient eighteen-year-old Amish girl.

She imagined she did. After all, she'd had a lot of

experience pretending she was just like everyone else. So far, no one had guessed anything different.

They were almost home when her mother spoke of Jackson. "I couldn't believe my eyes when I saw him," she murmured as their horse clip-clopped along the side of the road. "Truly, for a moment, I thought I might faint."

Even though Marie knew whom she was speaking of, she couldn't resist needling her. "Who?"

"You know, daughter. Jackson."

"It was a surprise." And that was the understatement of the year.

Still looking stunned, *Mamm* nodded. "We should not tell your father."

That was a given. He would get upset with them both for even saying his name. "I won't say a word to *Daed* about Jackson."

Her mother visibly relaxed. "*Gut.*" After the buggy traveled a few more yards, she added, "He…he looks like he's taken care of himself, though. He's turned into a fine-looking man. Ain't so?"

"He is handsome." Trying it on for size, she said, "He's *Englisch* now."

"*Jah*, he is. I expected he would be. He was never happy with the Amish way of life."

Marie couldn't help but disagree with that. Jackson seemed to have liked being Amish well enough. His faith had always seemed steady. No, his problem had been of a far more personal nature. He hadn't liked how awfully their father had treated him.

Another few minutes passed with Patty, their horse, trotting along in a steady manner like always. She was a smart horse. Marie never had to give her many signals in order to get home.

"Hopefully Jackson won't come back here again," *Mamm* blurted.

Marie didn't bother hiding her dismay. "Do you really hope that, *Mamm*? Do you really never want to see your son ever again?"

Her mother's face paled. For a second, it seemed as if she wasn't going to be able to catch her breath.

But then her expression hardened.

"He is not my son. I don't have a son."

"*Mamm*, you gave birth to him. You used to make him peanut butter cookies. Even I remember that."

"Don't speak of it. The Lord knows that I might have given him life but that man is not the baby I once held. He's forgotten."

Marie kept her further thoughts to herself but she knew that wasn't the truth.

Jackson might have been shunned. He might have been out of their lives for years and years...

But he wasn't forgotten. Not even a little bit.

Chapter Four

LizBeth had been so spun up after seeing Jackson at work she'd gone straight to her parents' house as soon as she closed the shop. Her parents lived in the family's large sprawling farmhouse. It had been in the Troyer family for four generations and easily resembled a mouse's maze. There was a large main house with five bedrooms, a medium-sized *dawdi haus* with two bedrooms, its own kitchen and living room, and even a large wing leading off to the side that her great-aunt Busy had always called the bride's walk.

Every time she stopped by, LizBeth felt a burst of nostalgia for the place. She, Frank and their two other siblings had played hide-and-seek in the rooms many, many nights. They'd also received almost as many stern lectures from Aunt Busy about bothering extended family members with their antics. Her aunt had been a ball of fire when she was in the store, but she'd loved peace and quiet at home.

LizBeth had elected to not be baptized in the Amish faith. Though her parents had been disappointed, they'd understood and encouraged LizBeth to go her own way.

She'd always been glad that her parents had been so understanding about the path she'd chosen to walk in life.

LizBeth imagined she'd always miss living in the big old house, however. Her snug apartment always felt slightly claustrophobic in comparison.

Lately, though, LizBeth was beginning to think that maybe her mother's kitchen felt confining as well.

"I don't think you should have anything to do with him," LizBeth's mother said over her cup of tea. "Jackson has been gone too long."

She'd been weighing the pros and cons of not only telling her mother about Jackson's sudden appearance but also his reason for visiting the store. Her whole family had been beside themselves with worry after he'd left without a single word for her. They'd hated how much he'd put her through.

She didn't blame them for their feelings, either. She had been upset, and his sudden disappearance had been alarming—not just for her but for the whole community.

However, everyone soon realized there did happen to be some people who did not act upset and distraught—such as his family. They had to have known something.

LizBeth's suspicions had been solidified when she'd paid a call to Myra Lapp with her mother, and Mrs. Lapp had pretended she didn't know who Jackson was. It had been obvious that his parents had decided to shun him.

It had been one of the most peculiar and aggravating conversations of her life. By the time they'd left and started the mile walk back home, her mother seemed to have changed her tune.

"I'm not sure what happened in that house, but whatever did had to have been terrible," her mother had said. "Myra never was good at lying, and she told a whale of a story today."

Returning to the present, LizBeth made a decision. "It seems Jackson is a policeman now. One of his cases brought him to the store."

"For what reason?"

"I don't know. I had customers when he showed up so we couldn't really talk."

"You couldn't ask Holden to take over things for a spell?"

"*Mamm*, Holden means well but we both know he's no Fern." Fern was a fifty-something Amish woman who had worked at Busy's for years and years. Though she had a tendency to always speak her mind and be rather judgmental, Fern was so competent that everyone joked she could run the whole town. LizBeth was simply glad that Fern liked her well enough. The woman could hold a mean grudge.

Looking bemused, her mother nodded. "Fern is mighty different from your cousin, for sure and for certain." After a pause, she added, "That's not a bad thing, though. Fern doesn't always make the right decisions, dear."

This was news to LizBeth. She wondered what her mother knew that she didn't. "Really? Since when?"

Mamm's expression closed up like a clamshell. "It's nothing for you to worry about, dear. I shouldn't have said anything." Injecting a decidedly peppy tone, she continued, "What matters far more is Jackson's return! Are you going to see him again? Or did you tell him to go bother someone else?"

Feeling like she was admitting a terrible offense, she said, "I'm seeing him tonight, *Mamm*."

"Tonight?" *Mamm* fairly squeaked.

"We're meeting at the Garden Goat Pizza Parlor. Jackson is going to tell me about the case then."

"I don't think that's a *gut* idea."

"I know, but it's necessary. This case he's working on seems awfully important, *Mamm*."

Still looking fretful, she said, "It might be, but you're important, too. You must consider the consequences, *jah*?"

"There are no consequences."

"Sure there are." She waved a hand. "I mean, what if something happens? He could hurt you."

"Jackson would never hurt me. He might be older, but he did not turn into his father."

"No, of course, he wouldn't lash out at you. But… what about your heart?"

Her mother was so perceptive. She cleared her throat. "My heart is perfectly safe from Jackson Lapp, *Mamm*. All I'm going to do is help him with a case."

Looking increasingly skeptical, she nodded. "I pray you are correct, dear. Though I feel I should warn you that though the heart is a muscle and protected by one's ribs, it is still a fragile thing."

"I'll keep it guarded. Of that you can be sure."

But instead of looking relieved, her mother only folded her arms across her chest and sighed.

LizBeth pretended not to notice.

Two hours later, she pulled up her Corolla in front of the Garden Goat in Millersberg. The hole-in-the-wall pizzeria was a community favorite and usually swarming with people. This evening was no exception.

She hoped the large crowd would serve their purpose. Neither of them would stick out in the crowd. Plus, there was a good chance that anyone who was Amish might not see them, since a lot of the Amish simply picked up a pizza and carried it home. They didn't stay to eat in the restaurant.

She'd taken her friend Ellen there each time she visited. She and Ellen had become close soon after LizBeth went out on her own. She'd accepted LizBeth from the start and helped make her transition to the *Englisch* world relatively easy.

LizBeth arrived five minutes early, hoping to find a table, but Jackson was already there. The hostess directed her to his table in the back corner. Jackson had his back to the wall and was facing the door, but a ball cap partially covered his eyes. From a distance, he didn't look any different from any other twenty-something man in the restaurant.

But maybe that was simply the truth. She was starting to get the feeling that maybe he really wasn't any different to most of the world. Only to her did he stand out.

He stood up when she approached. "Thanks for coming."

"I wouldn't have stood you up." She hadn't meant it in a degrading way, but he flinched.

"We should probably talk about the way I left, too."

"I didn't even see you leave Busy's." Well, she had, but she wasn't going to tell him that.

"LizBeth, I'm talking about how I left Berlin. And you."

His comment, so casually said, caught her off guard. "Your departure was a long time ago. Twelve years, remember?"

"I didn't forget."

"I don't see any reason to bring up our history now. I mean, you wanted to talk about your case, right?"

Jackson looked tempted to argue but held his tongue. "Right."

"Do you two know what you want?" the high school-aged server asked.

Jackson shook his head. "She just sat down. Can you give us a moment?"

"Yeah. Sure."

After he walked away, Jackson smiled at her. "I don't think he liked my answer."

"Probably not. There's usually a wait for tables."

"I guess we better decide on what we want, then. What do you usually get?"

"Nothing fancy. Just pepperoni."

"That sounds fine with me. Have you had the salads? Are they decent?"

"I have and they are good." Pointing to the cartoon drawing of the goat at the top of the menu, LizBeth added, "The couple who own the place have an organic goat farm. They also grow a lot of lettuce and such. Everything is really fresh."

"Really? I'll get a salad, too. And it's my treat. The department is paying for it."

"You seem awfully excited about that salad," she teased.

"When you're a cop, you eat out a lot, and half the time the meal is either something on the go or just a protein bar. I've learned to not eat too much junk."

"I hadn't thought about that." After the server came back and they placed their order, she leaned back. "Actually, Jackson, I'd say there are a lot of things about your life that have taken me by surprise."

"I feel the same way about seeing you." He paused, then added, "It's a good thing, though. I always wondered how you were."

"Really?"

"I knew when I left that I would probably be shunned. That kept me from asking too much, but I did think about everyone and wondered how they were doing. Especially you."

Especially her. Feeling like her mouth had just gone dry, she murmured, "Is that right?"

"Of course. I thought you would have gotten married by now. I never imagined that you would've left the church, too. When did that happen?"

Though her decision to not be baptized Amish wasn't a painful memory, she had no desire to speak of it at that moment. "That's a story for another day."

"Still, I wish I would've known that."

"Even if we could no longer have been together, we could have still kept in touch, Jackson. At the very least, you could've written me a letter after you left." Unable to help herself, she added, "Or any other time during the last twelve years."

"You're right. I could've." He looked beyond her, almost like he was staring into space. "I always promised myself not to second-guess the past. I think it's a mistake to compare the choices I made as a kid with my adult self."

"I reckon you're right."

"I know you don't want to talk about our past, but

I don't see how we can pretend it didn't happen." His blue eyes scanned her face. "I had to leave my house. I didn't have much choice. Not after that night we shared."

"I know. I mean, now I know. What are you going to do about your family? I know you practically ran into your mother and sister at the store."

"There's not much I can do. I might have grown up, but to them I still don't exist. At least, not to my parents."

Thankfully, their drinks arrived. Taking a large sip of her soda, LizBeth thought about Jackson's words and the way he seemed to regret cutting their ties. There was something in his tone that told her there was more to that story. She was interested in learning more…but not quite yet.

"Jackson, we should probably talk about the real reason you're here."

"I agree." He lowered his voice. "In a nutshell, a woman's body was found two years ago in a hotel room in Cincinnati." Looking even more somber, he added, "She'd been bound, violated and killed. Track marks were on her arms, signaling that someone had injected her with drugs. Under the cot was a bag holding her clothes, which included an Amish-looking dress and a white *kapp*."

She gasped. "Oh, my word."

Leaning a bit closer, he said, "LizBeth, all the clothes were in a canvas bag with a daisy embroidered on it."

"She had a Daisy Bag?" She knew she sounded incredulous, but it was so hard to believe.

Still looking pained, Jackson nodded. "At the time, no one knew what that meant. Since she didn't have any identification or medical records, she was eventually listed as a Jane Doe. Work on another case led me to this one. The moment I saw the photo of that canvas tote, I knew I had to take it on."

"So it might have been a woman from here."

"Yes."

"How old do you think she was?" When he hesitated, she pushed, "Was she older than me? Younger?"

"Younger."

"Much younger?" Boy, she hoped not.

Again, Jackson chose his words with care. "I wasn't at the scene, of course, but both the detective on the case and the coroner guess her age to be between sixteen and eighteen."

LizBeth felt as if she'd just been hit by a train. "So she was an Amish runaway."

"Maybe." He pursed his lips. "Or someone lured her away." Meeting her gaze again, he added, "I need to learn who she was so I can start retracing her steps and find out who murdered her."

"You need to speak to some other people besides me." Thinking quickly, she said, "Can you get a picture and pass it around? Someone might recognize her."

"I want to wait to do that. It's… Well, it's difficult to see."

Suddenly all kinds of awful scenarios came to mind. "How did she die? Was she shot?"

"No. It was a drug overdose."

"This is so awful. I want to help you, but I don't know what I can do." Unbending a little bit, she added, "Like you, I left the Amish community a decade ago."

"I've thought a lot about it, and I think I need to

visit the bishop. Do you know if Bishop Mark is still around?"

"He's not. Bishop Thaddaeus is here now."

"I see. What's he like?"

"Thad's a good man, but I don't know if he's going to tell you anything much."

"I doubt he will. He might not even know too much. But I need to figure out who this girl was. Only then am I going to be able to figure out who killed her."

She was prevented from replying by the arrival of both their pizza and his salad. After the server left, she smiled at him. "I still pray before I eat."

"I do, too." He closed his eyes and bent his head. She did the same.

When he raised his head, she said, "When we do things like that, it makes me feel like maybe we haven't drifted too far away from our roots."

"Funny, I was thinking that praying with you brought back a lot of memories." He unwrapped his silverware from the paper napkin enclosure. "I remember that you loved ice cream. Do you still?"

That was what he remembered? "I do, but I don't eat it too often now."

"Rocky Road?"

"That still is a favorite." Putting two slices on her plate, she said, "What about you? Do you still like Mountain Dew?"

He laughed. "No. It's actually been years since I've had soda. I'm more of a water and iced tea drinker now."

"Do you drink alcohol?"

He shook his head. "That never interested me. You?"

"Not me, either. Though I think that choice is

mainly because of that party. I never wanted to lose
control again."

"I felt the same way." He speared another big bite
of salad and munched.

"Where did you go when you ran? Did you know
someone?"

"Not at all. I ran to the highway and hitchhiked to
Cleveland. After spending the first night huddled on
the side of a building, I went to a fast-food place to
get breakfast and try to figure out what to do. A man
saw me, bought me a couple of egg McMuffins and
said I looked scared." He shook his head. "Next thing
I knew, I was telling him everything. He ended up
asking if I wanted to sleep in his guest bedroom for a
couple of nights."

"You trusted him?"

"My whole body was battered, I had ninety-two dollars to my name and was scared to death. I figured if
he was bad, I'd just leave out the window."

She felt like crying. Even though she was trying so
hard to keep at least a little bit of emotional distance
between them, his words were painful to hear. Oh,
she'd known that his parents had been harsh and that
he didn't get along with his father, especially.

She'd also seen some bruises on him from time to
time, but she always attributed them to all the work he
did on the farm.

But hearing Jackson speak of that time in such a
matter-of-fact way was eye-opening. *His body had
been battered.* That is what had happened to him.

He didn't just leave and find a new life. He ran into
a void and somehow, by his will and God's good grace,

he managed to survive. LizBeth struggled to contain her shock, but she doubted she did a very good job of it.

His smile revealed she was right. "It's okay, Liz-Beth. I know my actions sound farfetched."

"*Nee*, it's not that. It's just—well, I'm realizing that I was so focused on my own pain and confusion I didn't exactly think about what you endured. I'm sorry for that."

"There's nothing to be sorry for. I didn't know what I was jumping into, either." His eyes clouded. "I, too, was only thinking of myself. But that was a blessing, for sure and for certain. Otherwise, I don't know if I would have ever left."

"Was that man nice?"

"He was. Roy was the kindest man I ever knew. And not kind like hearts and flowers. Kind in the way that he had a big amount of patience for the dumb and confused boy I was back then. He mentored me in many things and even eventually helped me obtain my GED and enlist in the army."

"It's hard to imagine an Amish man joining the military."

"I know. At first, I wasn't sure what to do, but in the end it felt like the right path. Both God and Roy brought me to that path, which in turn brought me to the job I have now."

"Which brought you to that woman and back here."

"Yes. It seems I've gone full circle. It wasn't my intention, but I must surmise that it was the Lord's." He took a deep breath. "I will tell you this, though. All the pain I've been through and all the confusion and dismay I've felt since I've returned will be worth it if I can help that girl."

LizBeth realized Jackson was right. Yes, she'd felt his loss. Yes, he'd suffered far worse than she had since they'd separated. But neither of their stories mattered much when compared to the Amish girl who had been found.

"She's had no one to tell her story."

"No one until me, I guess." His expression hardened. "I mean to tell it, too. I'm not going to allow her to die in the middle of a strange city with all her belongings in an old daisy canvas tote bag. Someone needs to tell it. It might as well be me."

"I'll help you as much as I am able," she promised. There was no way she'd be able to simply stand aside or pretend that Jackson hadn't told her about his Amish Jane Doe.

"Thank you, LizBeth. That's all I'm asking. Just for you to try."

Later, long after they'd parted and she went to her small apartment, LizBeth thought about Jackson's words. He had been right. All that really needed to happen was for someone to care enough about the girl to try to help.

And right now, even the smallest effort was more than anyone had done for her so far.

Chapter Five

Two hours later, Jackson was on his way to see his sister. As he drove down the dark winding roads toward the Emersons' barn, part of him was shocked that nothing had changed. The roads were still narrow, winding, unmarked and unlit. The houses he passed were dark except for the occasional flickering light through a bedroom window or two.

There were still broad stretches of land in between homes, some fields filled with vegetation. Others looked abandoned and forgotten.

He'd even passed a pair of Amish boys walking on the side of the road. Only their white shirts had alerted Jackson to their presence. Neither of them had been carrying a flashlight or wearing any type of reflector. It had taken him off guard for a second—until he remembered that he'd walked along the side of the same roads in the middle of the night all the time. He'd thought he was invincible and would have scoffed at the idea of carrying any sort of flashlight.

The boys attempted to peer into Jackson's SUV win-

dow as he drove by. They'd obviously been looking to
see if they knew him.

If he'd stayed in Berlin, they probably would have.

So the journey was familiar. It was all as he remembered, but in some ways he was familiar with nothing
anymore. Not the darkness, nor the quiet.

His pace had quickened. He was used to vehicles
moving faster, modern conveniences at every turn,
and even a sense of disconnect with his surroundings.

Now in Cincinnati, he lived in a small two-bedroom
house that he'd bought three years ago. The house was
simple, but at the end of a cul-de-sac in a friendly sub-
division. A sidewalk took up part of his front yard and
the garage door had both a key code and an opener,
which was clipped to the visor in his car. Though he
didn't socialize much with his neighbors, he knew their
names and he said hello to them on the odd occasion
when they happened to be outside in their front yards.

And…that was the root of it all, he realized. What
was surprising *wasn't* that nothing had changed in
Holmes County. It was that he'd changed so much more.

Glancing at the glowing clock on the dashboard
of his vehicle, Jackson realized he was ten minutes
early for his meeting with Marie. Pleased about that,
he parked to the side, grabbed a flashlight from under
the seat and walked toward the barn.

Everything was quiet. Almost eerily still. Shining
his light into the woods nearby, he didn't even see or
hear the rustle of birds. The only noise was his thick-
soled boots pounding the hard dirt ground.

He stopped in front of the barn and saw that time
hadn't done the old structure any favors. The slats in
the sides of the barn had turned a lighter shade, looking

almost gray against the flashlight's beam. The boards were warped. A few gaped a bit, allowing wind, rain and no doubt more than a few enterprising bugs or rodents inside.

Walking to the door, he pulled. It opened easily, giving proof that while it might look to be abandoned by time, that wasn't the case. Someone—or multiple people—used the door on occasion.

His flashlight's beam revealed further proof of the barn's use. Eight or ten beer cans littered the floor, and what looked like a number of pizza boxes were stacked in a corner.

As were some clothes.

Walking to the pile, Jackson frowned. An Amish woman's dress was wadded up in a ball. He wondered if it had been accidentally left…or if it had been discarded on purpose. Could this place have something to do with his case…or was he so out of sorts from visiting his past that he was seeing trouble where there was nothing at all?

"Jackson?"

He turned to find Marie standing in the doorway of the barn. She had on a gray dress that was a little shorter than the norm, a white *kapp* and some ratty-looking white canvas tennis shoes. All the laces were gone. She held nothing in her hands.

Walking toward her, he felt his mouth go dry. At last, he was standing with Marie again. God was so good—he hadn't been sure if he'd ever get to do so again.

When she stood in front of him, instead of rushing toward his side, Jackson realized the two of them were a lot like the winding roads he'd just driven on. They were the same…but also very different.

When she continued to simply look at him, he said the first thing that came to mind. "Did you walk over here in the dark?"

Some of the curiosity in her eyes shuttered. "Obviously."

He'd offended her. Hating that he had hurt her feelings, he said, "You're in a gray dress. A car driving by might not have seen you."

Her chin lifted slightly. She was putting up with his comments, but only just. "There ain't no cars in the field, Jackson. I was fine. I am fine."

"Ah."

Looking a bit more confident, she walked into the space. Her eyes stayed focused on him. Sizing him up. It seemed she was just as anxious to look her fill as he'd been when he'd first spied her in the opening.

"It's good to see you, Marie," he finally said. "I should've said that the very first moment we talked. I'm so glad to see you—and you turned into such a beautiful woman, too."

"Hardly that."

"How about this, then? I've missed you."

She blinked, seemed to regain her composure. "It's *gut* to see ya, too."

"Did *Mamm* ask you about going out to the parking lot?"

"*Nee*. I'd lied to her and told her I had to go to the bathroom. She found me there."

"Oh. Good."

She turned slightly. "You needn't have worried. I've had a lot of practice sneaking around."

"I did, too, by the time I was your age."

"*Nee*, Jackson. By the time you were my age, you were gone."

"Yes, you're right." He attempted to smile. "I am glad you didn't get in trouble for talking to me."

"Me, too." She paused, seeming to weigh her words before continuing. "*Mamm* and I did talk about you on the way home, Jackson."

She'd moved away from him. Her body was now facing a tad to the right. They could see each other but weren't looking directly at one another. Jackson wondered if averting her eyes gave her a sense of security. He reminded himself that he did not want to be a source of discomfort for her. No matter what, he loved his little sister and ached for her to trust him.

"Hey, Marie, do you still want to talk?" he asked gently. "We can discuss anything you'd like."

"Of course I do." She looked him in the eye again. "That's why I came."

Progress! "I don't know where to go. Should we sit down on the floor?"

She giggled. "You're such a city boy now. Of course, we're gonna just sit on the floor, but turn off the flashlight."

"You don't think it would be better to see each other?" And to get a good eyeful of whoever might join them.

She rolled her eyes, once again looking every inch a teenager. "Your fancy flashlight is going to tell anyone passing that we're in here. We can't do that, right?"

"Fine." Deciding not to remind her that his vehicle parked off to the side would be the sure giveaway, Jackson turned off the light, enfolding them in darkness. "Better?"

"Jah."

Slowly, his eyes adjusted and he could see her small, slight form sitting on the ground. She had her arms wrapped around her knees and her head was resting on them. In the shadows, she looked younger and more fragile. But, of course, that was what she was. Marie might think she was an enlightened, worldly eighteen-year-old girl, but Jackson knew different. She was just a sheltered young woman pretending to be someone she was not.

It was just like how he had been.

Deciding to start with something nonthreatening, he said, "How did you know about this barn?"

"What do you mean? Everyone comes up here."

"Even you?"

"Of course even me." She laughed softly. "Maybe I should say especially me."

Marie might be older and practically a stranger, but he recognized that slight hitch in her voice. "Why is that?"

Her voice darkened. "Why do you think, Jackson?"

"I don't know," he said honestly. "As you've pointed out, I've been gone a long time. When I left, you were only six. Now you're almost grown up."

"Not *almost.* I've been out of school for four years now. I did grow up."

"You're still only eighteen."

"Don't act like that means I'm a child." Her chin lifted. "You know as well as I do that some girls my age are already married."

"Do you have a beau?"

"Not really. I wish I did, though," she said in a bitter

tone. "Being married would be a lot better than being home all the time."

"You're home that much?"

"For sure." Bitterness laced her words. "Our father don't trust anyone outside of the house to be around me."

Though his parents had kept an old order household, their father had grown up *Swartzentruber*, which was by far the most conservative branch of the Amish. Most *Swartzentruber* Amish didn't allow their wives or daughters to work outside the home. "How is he?" Jackson finally asked.

She sighed. "He's the same, Jackson."

Same? "Has he beaten you?"

"Not like he used to beat you."

"But he has?" Guilt filled him. Why hadn't he realized this?

"What do you think? Since you aren't around and there ain't no one else, I'm his number one choice." Her voice turned fainter. "Next to *Mamm*."

Jackson felt sick to his stomach. How could he have been so selfish? Why hadn't he done something more for his sister besides pray for her? "I had hoped *Daed* had gotten better."

"If you thought it was possible, then you are either really stupid or somewhere in your travels you learned to have really high hopes."

Jackson was shocked by how harsh she seemed. Even though he knew she'd grown up, there had always been something about her that was innately sweet and gentle. He wondered if his leaving had made her this way. "I don't know what to say. He seemed to always focus on me. I thought with me gone, *Daed* would've calmed down."

She sighed. "Even if it ain't wonderful at home, you are right. It isn't as bad as when you were there."

At least that was something. "I am sorry for abandoning you, Marie. But, ah, since we're being so honest, I have to tell you that your needs were the furthest thing from my mind."

"Because *Daed* had hurt you bad that night."

Forgetting they were in the dark and she couldn't see, he nodded. Then he made himself say the words. "He did. I was badly hurt. He said I was going to get it worse the next day. I had no reason not to believe him."

"*Mamm* likes to pretend that you never existed, but both she and him were real shaken up when they'd realized you left."

"I don't think it ever occurred to them that I might not want to stay on the farm." Practically feeling her stare burning into him, he said, "Like I said, I am sorry that things aren't better."

"Maybe instead of us just talking about the past, you can tell me why you've come back."

There was hope in her voice. In a sudden flash of insight, he realized that she had never given up on him. Even though he'd taken off in the middle of the night, never left her a note, never tried to contact her—she was still hopeful that he hadn't forgotten her.

She was hoping he'd come to take her away.

If he could have dug a hole and hidden himself in shame, he would have. "Marie, I'm a policeman now. I do a lot of things on my job, but what I mainly do now is try to solve homicides. Murders," he explained, in case she wasn't familiar with the word. "I came back to Berlin to try to solve a murder."

"Oh."

He felt even worse. "Marie, I'm not going to lie to you. I didn't come here to rescue you. I thought you were fine and probably had forgotten about me. Or hated me because of what I did."

"I don't even know what you did."

"I'll be happy to tell you, but not now."

"All right, then." She moved to stand up.

He scrambled to his feet. "Hey, hold on! I'm not done, Marie."

"I think I'm done listening. I don't reckon you've got anything more to say that I want to hear."

"How about this? How about I tell you that I'm single, I'm *Englisch* and I live about three hours south of you. I've got a job that takes me all around a big city and I spend the majority of my time talking to people who might have committed murder." After seeing that he had her attention, he took a deep breath. "All that said... I'll be happy to take you home with me."

"For how long?"

"Forever." Jackson meant that, too. He might have made a hundred mistakes where she was concerned, but it wasn't too late to begin making amends.

"Forever's a long time, Jackson."

"Okay, how about this? You may stay with me as long as you want, Marie. Stay with me until you feel comfortable and are ready to do something on your own."

"Just like that?"

He supposed he deserved the derision in her tone. "Think about it."

She stood up, then. "I don't need to. Besides, I've

got another way out of here and he doesn't act like I'm not worth his time."

Feeling the skin on the back of his neck tingle, he got to his feet. "He? Is he the kind of boyfriend you mentioned?"

"*Nee*, he's better than that. He helps Amish girls who want to leave get out."

He. Amish girls. Not Amish teens. Red flags were going up with practically every word. "Who is this man?" he asked urgently. "What's his name?"

"I'm not going to tell you. You're a cop."

He strode toward her. Only harsh memories of their father grabbing him kept Jackson from reaching for her. "Marie, I need to know his name."

"Why, Jackson?" she asked softly. "Is it because you're worried about me...or because you think it might help your murder?"

"Both," he said before he realized that it would have been better to lie.

She turned so her back was facing him. "I've gotta go."

"No, don't do that. Stay and talk to me."

"I've gotta go or I'll be missed."

"Hold on. At the very least, let me take you home."

"No way. And you won't be driving me near the house, either. *Mamm* or *Daed* would see the headlights a mile away."

"Fine. I'll walk you home."

"*Nee*, Jackson!"

"Then see me again," he said urgently. When she remained silent, he added, "Marie, if you want, pretend that I didn't leave, that our parents aren't horrible and I haven't become a cop you don't trust. If nothing else, just think of the truth."

"Which is what?"

"That you are my little sister and I love you."

"Jackson..."

"See me again soon, Marie," he said quickly. "Even if you never want to see me again in the future, at least give me that. Please."

Her shoulders slumped. "All right. Fine."

"Thanks. When?"

"In three nights' time?"

He'd planned to already be back home by then. He pushed back that thought. "Fine. Here again?"

"*Jah.* There ain't nowhere else to go, Jackson. I'll see you then."

"At eleven."

She nodded. "And just to make sure about things, hear me say this. Come alone."

"I'll be here alone at eleven."

As she opened the door, the faint light from the moon cast a beam on her face. She smiled. "*Gut.*"

Then she turned around and darted off.

Two minutes later, when he glanced outside, she was long gone.

Chapter Six

Even though she'd been on her feet all day, LizBeth went for a walk when she got home from work. She had too much to think about and too many questions she needed answers to. If she sat home and stewed, she knew all she'd get was a headache. She'd never completely learned how to relax. Sitting on the couch and reading a book or watching television had never appealed to her.

Since the air was a slightly cool sixty degrees, she pulled on a sweatshirt. Right before she walked out the door, she grabbed a ten-dollar bill, her keys and her phone. If she was up for it, she could walk all the way to the Dairy Dip. It was a little over a mile from her home, but the prospect of an orange-and-vanilla-swirled cone always made her feet move a little quicker.

Feeling pleased about her decision to get out of the house, LizBeth forced herself to think about Jackson as she walked down her apartment's back stairs. Boy, but he was still handsome. Still handsome and still so good.

Oh, sure. He was a man now. And he had a whole lot more hard edges than he'd had when they'd both been teenagers. But she'd recognized that same burst of compassion in his expression that she'd often seen when he'd looked at his little sister.

And her.

He was still a good man.

LizBeth could be wrong, but she was pretty sure there was still something between them, too. Her *Englisch* friends would call it chemistry. There was something connecting them still and she knew it wasn't just memories of their past. She'd even spied Jackson staring at her lips for a second when they'd sat across from each other in the booth at Garden Goat.

Maybe he, too, was remembering the way he used to hold her in his arms and kiss her until they'd scarcely been able to breathe. She'd clung to him like he was the best thing in her life and returned his kisses like she'd die without them.

Feeling her skin flush, LizBeth had to laugh at herself. Maybe Jackson's kisses had been her addiction. They'd certainly encouraged her to do things she'd never thought she would.

The blare of church bells jerked her out of the memories. Hastily, she answered the phone before glancing at the screen. "Hello?"

"You answered on the first ring. I'm going to take that as a good sign," Donny said in her ear.

Donny. She'd recently begun to chat with him at church. He'd made it plenty clear that he was interested in her and wanted to get to know her better. He seemed nice, really nice. He was easy to talk to and well-liked by everyone in the congregation. Some women had even hinted they were a little envious about how Donny had zeroed in on LizBeth.

Since she still had moments of doubts about herself, she couldn't deny that Donny's attention was flattering. However, she simply wasn't sure if she wanted to date him. On paper, he was everything she could ask for. Reasonably handsome, employed, faithful. Nice to puppies.

But there was no spark. Of late, she'd imagined that the reason she'd never been attracted to Donny didn't have as much to do with him as herself. Maybe she simply wasn't capable of feeling passionate about much anymore.

But now, after seeing Jackson again, LizBeth realized the truth. It wasn't that she wasn't capable of feeling sparks; it was that Donny wasn't Jackson. For better or worse, she had to admit there was still something about Jackson that made her heart beat a little bit faster.

She forced a chuckle. "You called at a good time. I was out walking. How are you?"

"I'm good. I just got home from working out." His voice warmed. "You know, you should join me sometime. It would be great."

Even if she did want to go to a gym to work out, she certainly didn't want to go with a guy. That would feel like putting herself into a vulnerable space—especially if he had anything to say about her body. "Thanks, but I don't think I'm up for that."

"Are you sure? If you help your body, you'll help your state of mind, too. Maybe you'll even learn to relax a little bit."

LizBeth frowned. It was comments like this that made her think twice about seeing Donny socially. She didn't want to hear his opinions about what she should be doing.

"I'm sure," she said lightly.

"All right. Well, I guess I shouldn't be worried about you, anyway. You're gorgeous the way you are."

She rolled her eyes. "Was there any special reason you called?"

"Yes. LizBeth, here's the deal. We've been talking for a while. Everyone at church has noticed."

"They have?"

He laughed softly. "You know how everyone is at church—everyone loves seeing two members hit it off."

She honestly didn't think their conversations had drawn much notice. "Donny, I'm not sure we've garnered much attention."

"I promise you, we have. I think it's time we moved forward. We should finally go out on a proper date."

There it was again—something in the way he said things that made her want to shrink back from him. "Finally?" she murmured.

"You know what I mean, LizBeth. We've been talking to each other for months at church. If everyone else has noticed my attention, you have to have noticed as well."

Feeling more uncomfortable by the second, she said, "We have been talking for a while, that's true. But I thought we were just friends." Okay, that was kind of a lie, but she didn't like how Donny was acting like she should be so grateful for his attention.

"There's a restaurant in Walnut Creek that I've been meaning to try out. Josephine's Café. How about we head there on Saturday night?"

"I'm sorry but Saturday night's not good for me. I have plans."

"What are you doing?"

His pushy ways were helping her make her decision. "I've got an old friend in town. We've made tentative plans to see each other. I'm afraid I can't break them."

"Your plans are that important? Why? Where are you going?"

"I'm not sure. He said he was going to let me know."

"He? You're seeing a man."

She rolled her eyes. "Yes."

"I think I get it now."

She hoped so. It wasn't until right this minute that she realized the two of them wouldn't ever work out. Donny was too pushy, too assertive and too intrusive. She was in no hurry to spend hours alone with him if he was going to be like that.

"Thanks for calling, Donny."

"Bye, LizBeth."

Hearing his click, she smiled to herself. She absolutely could have handled things with him better. Her mother, had she overheard the conversation, would have clucked in disapproval. She did not believe in any sort of lying at all. And LizBeth's clumsy, evasive maneuvers would be considered lying.

But at the moment, she didn't care. All that mattered was that she wasn't going to have to figure out what to do about Donny anytime in the near future. From the way he'd ended the conversation, she was fairly certain he had no intention of asking her out again. Given the relief she felt, she knew that was a very good thing.

When her phone buzzed again, she glanced down at the screen in surprise. "Hi, Jackson."

"Hey. Are you busy?"

"Not so much. I'm out for a walk. Why?"

"It looks like I'm going to be here for a couple more

nights. I was wondering if you would go to dinner with me sometime soon."

"When?"

"Anytime," he said with a laugh. "Tonight, tomorrow, the next night…"

"I'm not sure whether I should be flattered or you're just really bored."

He hesitated. "How about if we just keep it at this— I could use a friend right now and you're the best one I have here."

She smiled. No, his comment wasn't especially charming or flattering. But it was honest and maybe even sounded a little raw, a little desperate. That appealed to her, she realized.

"I was kidding about being flattered. I'd like to join you for supper."

"Yeah?"

He sounded so pleased she couldn't help but grin. "Yeah. How about tomorrow night?"

"Tomorrow night's perfect. Can I pick you up? You can choose where to go."

"That sounds good." After relaying her address, she asked, "Is six o'clock too early for you?"

"Not at all. Besides, we're in Amish country. Everything will be shutting down at seven."

That was the truth. "I'll look for you at six, then."

"Thanks, LizBeth."

Jackson sounded so relieved she wondered what had happened. "Is anything wrong? I mean, beyond the fact that you're trying to hunt down a murderer?"

"I had a conversation with Marie last night. She… Well, she didn't exactly give me a warm welcome. I didn't expect one, but…" He cleared his throat. "You know, never mind. I think it's pretty obvious that I should've thought things through."

"I can't speak for your sister, but I can share that if you give someone time to adjust, they can surprise you. She'll come around."

"Do you really think there's a chance?"

"Think of what's happened between the two of us, Jackson. Just a couple days ago I was sure I never wanted to see you again."

"And now you've agreed to go out to a second meal with me."

"I'm just saying that sometimes it's easier to guard one's heart than to be vulnerable."

"I can understand that. No one wants to be hurt."

"I've always felt that people will do a lot of things in order to avoid pain. Sometimes it might make a person do quite a few things they never dreamed they'd do."

"I think you're right, LizBeth. I'll see you tomorrow. Thanks."

After they clicked off, LizBeth turned around and headed back home. In the span of thirty minutes, she'd been asked out twice by two very different men. It seemed she'd made her choice, too.

Even though she and Jackson might never be anything more than distant friends, she had a feeling she'd made the right decision.

What was surprising was that it seemed she'd been speaking about herself when she said a person would do a lot to avoid pain. It was either that or let hope get in the way. And she prayed she wasn't just being a foolish woman with too much optimism for a man who didn't deserve it.

Chapter Seven

Jackson had spent the last twenty-four hours reac-
quainting himself with Berlin and the surrounding
areas. He visited the local sheriff's department and
introduced himself to Sheriff Mose Kramer. Mose was
an easygoing fellow in his late forties who had also
been brought up Amish but had jumped the fence.

After inquiring about Jackson's Amish Jane Doe
case, Mose shared some information about the under-
ground groups who supposedly helped Amish teens
run away. According to Mose, some of the groups had
nothing but the teenagers' best interests in mind. Others, on the other hand, did very little out of the good-
ness of their hearts. And those groups were also far
more secretive and distrustful of cops.

Seeking to get someone in authority on Jackson's
side, Mose reached out to one of his old neighbors. He
was able to arrange a meeting between Jackson and
a bishop of one of the largest church districts for that
very afternoon.

All those conversations took time and were important to the case. That wasn't a surprise. What he was

surprised about was how much time he spent down memory lane. It seemed every building, field and intersection brought back a new wave of memories. Some were fond, while others were a little more painful.

Jackson realized that much of Berlin was exactly how he remembered but other parts were far different. He discovered that some of his memories had been made through a teenager's sheltered view of the world. Stores and buildings that he'd remembered being vast were far smaller, just as men and women whom he'd been wary of now seemed just full of bluster.

That hindsight perception caught him a bit off guard—and it also made him wonder how his mature self might view his tumultuous teenage years. He was fairly sure he would have felt pity for the boy he'd been.

He was just sitting down at a table in the back of a diner with a number of missing-persons files from the last few years when Sergeant Phillip Gunther, his sergeant from the Cincinnati PD, called.

"Detective Lapp," he said when he answered.

"Jackson, tell me you've gotten some information," his sergeant said without preamble.

"Some. It's taking time, though. Is everything all right?"

The older man sighed. "It is and it isn't. The old manufacturing plant off of Lowell burned down yesterday. Two homeless men were in it. At first the fire investigator figured it was an accident but now there's evidence of tampering. He thinks there's a good chance it was arson."

"Oh, no. Any leads?"

"Only about a dozen. We need you back, Jackson."

"I understand, sir, but I need to follow through with

a couple of leads I've found." Of course, that was putting a positive spin on what was actually happening, but it was still the truth. He needed to be here. Needed to help his sister. Needed to understand what was going on with this guy Marie had spoken of…and he also needed to see where his relationship with LizBeth was going to go.

"How much time do you need?"

"At least through the weekend. Maybe even a couple more days." Practically able to feel his sergeant's annoyance rise, he added, "I can take personal days if you need me to."

"Jackson, what is going on, really?"

He'd never said much about his youth. There was no reason to do that. But maybe the right time to share his past had come. "I grew up here, Phillip."

"I realize that."

"No, what I'm trying to say is that I grew up Amish here. I left in the middle of the night when I was a teenager and haven't been back since."

"Are you serious?"

"Absolutely. I wouldn't joke about this." Taking a breath, he added, "My sister is eighteen and I fear she knows something, but it's taking a minute for her to trust me again."

"You haven't stayed in touch?"

"I've been shunned. As far as my parents believe, I'm dead to them."

"Wow." He paused. "You have until Sunday. I want you to report back on Monday morning. Understand?"

"Yes, sir."

"I mean it. I feel bad for this Amish Jane Doe, but the case has been cold for two years now."

"I understand. I'll be back on Monday."

"Good enough."

Sensing that Phillip was about to hang up, Jackson added, "Sir, thanks for understanding."

"Thanks for being upfront with me. Family is important. Roots are, too. Even if you don't want to connect with either, a man can't pretend they don't exist. They're always there."

"I'm finding that out. Thanks again."

"Later," the sergeant said before disconnecting.

That illuminating conversation rang in his head as he knocked on Bishop Thad's door an hour later. As much as he'd thought his past was erased, he realized that it had faded but never completely gone away.

His mouth went dry as the door opened, revealing a petite woman with blond hair faded to a bright gray. She had on a dark navy dress with a matching apron, a pristine white *kapp* and really pretty dark brown eyes. They seemed to twinkle when she smiled at him.

"Jackson Lapp, I presume?"

"Yes. I have an appointment with Bishop Thad."

"Thaddeus is in the back. He's been looking forward to chatting with you." As she started down the hall, she looked back at him and smiled again. "I'm Mary, by the by."

"It's nice to meet you. Thank you for allowing me to come over."

"Don't be silly, Jackson. We're happy to help."

As he followed her down the hall, it occurred to him that she wasn't referring to anything in particular. She was simply opening her home for a visit because he'd asked. It was humbling to witness, especially for someone like himself, who had left the faith so long ago.

"Here we are. Thad, your guest is here," Mary called out.

Bishop Thadeus was sitting by a fire. Unlike most people he came across, the man wasn't reading, working on a crossword or playing on a phone. He was simply sitting in the quiet. Seemingly at peace.

At Mary's announcement, he got to his feet and crossed the room to greet Jackson. "Hello, I am Bishop Thaddeus, but everyone calls me Thad."

"Hi, Thad. I'm Detective Jackson Lapp, but everyone calls me Jackson."

Thad smiled. "I'm pleased to make your acquaintance." He looked to Mary. "Any chance we could have some *kaffi*?"

"Of course." Sending another smile their way, she turned and walked down the hall.

"Come in and have a seat," Thad said. "I must admit that I was intrigued to hear from you."

"I imagine it's not often that a Cincinnati detective asks for your time."

"I'd agree with that, to be sure. But I was referring mainly to you, seeing how you're from around these parts and all."

Later, he'd wonder why he'd been so taken by surprise, but at the moment he could hardly do more than gape. "You know of my name?"

"I've heard tales of a young man by the name of Jackson Lapp leaving one night without so much as a backward glance. I can only surmise that you are one and the same."

"You're right." He swallowed the lump that had just

formed in his throat. "I did leave years ago." When Thad merely nodded but didn't say anything, he added, "Would you rather not speak to me?"

"I didn't say that, did I?" Looking just beyond him, Thad smiled. "*Danke*, Mary. Your *kaffi* and cookies will hit the spot."

Seeing Mary approach with a wooden tray laden with two cups of coffee and a small plate of cookies, Jackson stood up to help her. She gave it to him easily and then turned back around without a word.

"Have a cookie, Jackson, and stop worrying so. There's nothing wrong with me knowing your past— or with you owning it. One can change a lot of things, but not what's already happened, ain't so?"

"*Jah*." He sipped the coffee, which was dark and rich. Surprisingly good. "I'm actually here for your help." He briefly shared the story about Jane Doe and the Daisy Bag. "So you see, I need to know about any girls in the area who might have left two years ago."

"Of course, that would be hard to know about. Things like that aren't discussed."

"I know. But she deserves to have her case closed. Just because it might be uncomfortable for a family, doesn't mean that what happened should be ignored."

Thad raised his eyebrows. "I canna argue with that."

He took another long sip of coffee before speaking again. "Two years is a bit ago. There might be a woman or two who come to mind, but I ain't sure if I have the time right or not."

Though Jackson hadn't imagined that the bishop would immediately have a name for him, he had hoped he would be more helpful. Trying another tack, he said, "Have you heard any information about a man meeting with Amish teens who want to leave the faith against their parents' wishes?"

"Why do you ask?"

Jackson's senses shot up. "A young girl has told me there's such a man in the area. She led me to believe he's had some success."

Thad rubbed his beard. "I'm fairly sure that that's just talk, Jackson." He leaned back in his chair. "You know how teenagers are. They like to make up tales. Not all of them are true, though."

"You think this story is a tale?"

"Of course." He stood up. "I'm not saying this girl made it up, but I would caution you to take her words with a grain of salt, *jah*? We have a warm, loving community. We raise our *kinner* and help them adopt the values that we and our fathers and their fathers had. There's no need for anyone to have to sneak away in order to jump the fence."

Jackson believed Bishop Thad was an honest, faithful man. He had a feeling he was a treasured member of the community and had given a great many people a wealth of support in times of trial.

But he also was fairly sure that Thad was keeping something from him.

"Thank you for seeing me. I appreciate your time, and the coffee and cookies, too."

Looking relaxed again, the bishop held out his hand for Jackson to shake. "I'm glad I could help. I imagine you can see yourself out now."

"Of course." He turned and walked down the hall. When he passed the kitchen, Mary's back was to him. He paused. "Thank you for the hospitality, Mary."

Only a small nod let him know that she'd heard.

He let himself out the same door he'd entered and slowly walked to his car. He didn't think he'd just made an enemy, but he did have the feeling that he'd somehow encountered a roadblock. A very sturdy, immovable one.

Jackson hoped and prayed he wasn't going to have to make an enemy out of the bishop in order to discover what really happened to his Amish Jane Doe.

But, of course, that thought led to another trite phrase that Bishop Thaddaeus might have easily spouted: Wishes and dreams were for fools.

Chapter Eight

It was ironing day at the Lapp house. Specifically, ironing-the-sheets day, which was Marie's least favorite day of the week. Heating hot irons, holding them with thick rags and smoothing them over the worn cotton took a great amount of concentration and a steady hand. One moment of indecision could scorch the fabric, resulting in a lecture from her mother. It would also mean that she would have to sew another sheet and press it perfectly.

Or her father would find out.

When she was younger, she'd been shocked to discover that none of her girlfriends' families ironed sheets. Honestly, several had thought it was a mighty odd thing to worry about. Though Marie privately agreed, she also realized it didn't matter if she cared about pressed sheets or not. All that mattered was that her father had requested such a thing, and so it was to be done.

Standing in the kitchen, sweating from the heat of the hot irons, Marie carefully smoothed the white fabric. She'd only completed one sheet and she had another three to go, plus six pillowcases. "I really hate this," she mumbled under her breath. "I hate this, and I hate Jackson, too."

Realizing what she'd blurted, she hastily set the hot iron back on the stove and begged the Lord for forgiveness.

The truth was that she didn't hate Jackson at all. She loved him. She just *wanted* to hate her brother. But she didn't. She wished she understood all the emotions swirling around inside her.

Jah, she had so many disturbing, conflicting emotions where her long-lost brother was concerned, Marie hardly knew what to think or do. On one hand, she resented him for leaving her. He'd been her lifeline when she was small. She'd looked up to him and had been sure he could do no wrong.

When he left, she'd been so confused and scared. For years, she'd blamed herself, certain she had done something to help drive him away. However, it had turned out that she only needed to be a bit older to completely understand how angry and cruel their father could be. With each passing year, he'd demanded more perfection—while the consequences of not living up to his expectations had gotten more severe. Sometimes, in her weakest moments, Marie would even wonder if their father had done something awful to Jackson. She couldn't think of another reason why her brother hadn't even written her a letter.

That had been a sin to think, of course, but she'd prayed for forgiveness.

Marie had also prayed that the Lord would bring Jackson back to her, somehow or some way. Eventually, as each year passed without a word from him, Marie's faith began to waver. She couldn't understand why God had ignored all her prayers and cries.

But it seemed He had listened to her, after all. It had just been His timing, not hers.

Mixed in with all her distrust and confusion was love for her brother. And maybe—just maybe—a bit of pride, too. Jackson had done the unthinkable. He'd left on his own and not only survived but flourished. He'd become a strong, caring man. A police officer who solved crimes. He'd become everything all the elders liked to whisper would never happen to any-one who left.

She was also afraid of him. Oh, not that he would physically harm her. No, she was afraid of something far worse—that she'd grow to depend on Jackson. Or that she'd allow herself to believe his promises…and then he'd disappear again. If that happened, she'd be left feeling even more alone.

"Marie?" *Mamm* called out from the sewing room. "What are you doing?"

Hastily, she put down the iron she was holding. "I'm ironing, *Mamm*. You know that."

"How many sheets have you finished?"

"One. Almost two."

"You'd best hurry. Your father will be home for din-ner soon. He won't want you in the kitchen ironing while he eats."

"I'll hurry." She would, too, though she really didn't think it was fair that she had to rush through the task because her father liked the kitchen to be spotless and empty while he ate.

Picking up another hot iron, Marie began to smooth it as quickly as possible over the pure white sheet. Each wrinkle and crease vanished. Five minutes later, the second sheet was done.

"I'm never going to iron another sheet after I leave here," she whispered to herself. "Aaron won't make me do such things. I'm sure of it."

"Who are you speaking to?"

Startled, the iron slipped from her hand and landed on the sheet with a thud. A faint sizzle erupted. She gasped as she reached for the iron and picked it up without a towel.

"Marie!"

Her name registered the same moment the pain in her hand reached her brain. She dropped the iron again, this time on the floor. Barely three inches from her toes. She cried out and jumped.

"Oh!" *Mamm* yelled as she rushed forward.

"I'm okay," Marie murmured, right as she realized that her mother was on her hands and knees, inspecting the floor for a scorch mark. "Is the floor burned?"

"*Nee.* Not that I can tell, at least." Struggling to her feet, she grabbed a cloth and picked up the iron with a sigh. "You must be more careful, Marie. The floor was almost ruined."

"I know."

"And the sheet!" She picked up the sheet and inspected it like it was an expensive linen napkin or dress. There was a two-inch dark mark in the center. "I fear you've ruined another one, Marie." *Mamm* glanced warily at the door. "We better clean this up before your father returns."

Marie picked up one of the cooled irons and carried it to the stationary tub next to the back door. For a second, she was tempted to run cold water over her blistered hand, but she didn't dare. Instead, she pretended it didn't throb.

When she returned for the next one, she found her mother folding the ruined sheet. "*Mamm*, do you ever get tired of doing all these things just because *Daed* wants them done a certain way?"

"Your father wants them done the right way, Marie."

"I don't know anyone else who irons sheets. Why do we?"

"You know why. Sheets look better ironed."

"But don't you think it's a waste of time?" Not to mention a waste of energy and worry.

"Don't say such things."

"But—"

After glancing at the window again, her mother glared at her. "It is what it is, daughter! Now, help me clean your mess up and get dinner on the table. If we don't have it ready when he arrives, we're both going to be sorry."

"*Jah, Mamm*." Feeling guilty, she grabbed the rest of the pillowcases and hurried to put them all in a cupboard. Next, she neatly placed three quilted place mats on the table and brought over the pitcher of water and glasses while her mother raced around the kitchen.

Ten minutes later, she was standing next to her mother when her father entered the room. Immediately, his eyes scanned every corner, looking for flaws. *Mamm* inhaled when *Daed* studied the kitchen floor for crumbs or dirt.

"What is for dinner, Myra?" he asked at last.

"Breaded chicken with vegetables."

"Is it ready now?"

"It is."

He sat down with a sigh. "*Gut.*"

As Marie carried the bowl of mashed potatoes to the table, she pretended her palm wasn't on fire. Pretended she was hungry when she wasn't. Pretended this wasn't just another bad day in a string of many bad days.

After she sat down, took care to hide her blistered palm and ate her food, Marie made plans to get away soon.

Anything had to be better than this. Anything at all.

Chapter Nine

It had taken some time, but LizBeth had found an old list of Daisy Bag recipients that her grandmother had insisted be compiled. It was in a large spiral notebook with three columns written neatly in ballpoint pen. In it was the name of the recipient, the date the bag was given and a short note about why it was given.

Busy had certainly made a big fuss about the presentation of each bag. When LizBeth had been younger, she'd privately made fun of the presentation. She'd told her friends that her *mommi* always acted as if each bag were a grand prize in a drawing or worth a thousand dollars.

To her shame, she'd also resented the way her grandmother had insisted each name, date and other information be written down meticulously. Sometimes a whole line of people had to wait while the notebook was filled out and she hated having to make anyone wait.

But now it seemed that she'd been the one who was wrong. The notebook was going to be invaluable to Jackson. Or at the very least, he'd have a starting point.

She'd sent Jackson a text that morning and asked him to stop by the store. They had a date that evening, but LizBeth didn't want to wait to give him the list of names. Yes, things between them weren't exactly smooth sailing, but that didn't mean she didn't want to give him as much help to solve his case as possible.

Thankfully, the shop was empty when he entered. He was on the phone when he walked through the door but disconnected when she smiled at him.

"Hey," he said as he slipped it into a pocket of his blazer.

He looked as handsome as ever in his blazer, T-shirt, jeans and boots. Trying not to notice that he also smelled good, she said, "Hiya. Thanks for coming over. I found a notebook my grandmother saved that I think you can use."

"LizBeth, that's great. Really great." His expression became all business. "Do you have it handy?"

"Of course." Picking up the broad notebook off the counter, she handed it to him. "I hope it will help."

Instead of clutching it to him, Jackson opened the notebook to the middle and skimmed the page. Almost immediately, he picked it up and studied it more intently. "I can't believe this." Glancing up at her, he added, "Busy wrote down every recipient and the date?"

"Without fail."

"This must have taken a lot of time to catalog everything."

"I suppose." LizBeth shrugged. "Like we've said, your victim might have simply received that bag from one of the women on the list, but at least it's a start."

"Did your grandmother have any special requirements for deciding who the recipients were?"

She thought about that. "Not really. Sometimes she gave them to the best customers of the month. Other times because a woman was special to her and she gave it to her on the date of her baptism." LizBeth thought some more, searching her memories for something that might be of use to Jackson. "The only thing I can remember that might help is that *Mommi* never gave a bag to someone who asked for one. Or tried to buy one. She would really never give one to a random tourist."

"Really?"

LizBeth smiled. "Busy had a couple of quirks, I guess. But we all do, ain't so?"

"Indeed." Running a finger down more entries, he added, "Thank you. This list helps a lot."

Since there were hundreds of names, she wondered how it would be helpful. "What will you do with this list?"

"I'm going to look at the reasons that were listed. Maybe we can sit with your family and they can help me eliminate some of the women."

"I'm sure my family will help you. They'd be glad to."

He smiled at her. "Thanks, LizBeth."

Returning the smile, she felt her cheeks flush with pleasure—until she realized that she was likely gazing at him like a love-struck fool.

Gazing at him like she used to do.

"Like I said, I hope it helps."

He closed the notebook and tucked it under his arm. "I'm sure it will." He paused. "Would you still like to go out to eat tonight?"

"I was planning on it." Realizing she sounded too

eager, she amended, "I mean, I think it sounds like fun. If you would still like to go, that is."

"I still do." He smiled. "After all, with me being in that motel room, I need to eat somewhere, right?"

"Oh. Right." The bell at the shop's door chimed as a group of customers came in. Relieved, she waved a hand. "*Wilcom.* Please let me know if you need any help."

One of the women marched over to her. "Someone I know got a cute little canvas bag from here years ago. It has a daisy embroidered on it. Do you still give those out?"

"Occasionally."

"Well, I'd like one, please."

"I'm sorry, they're not for sale."

The bossy woman raised her eyebrows. "That's fine. I didn't intend to pay for it."

Feeling Jackson's gaze on her, LizBeth shook her head. "*Nee,* what I mean is that they are only given to special customers. Some of the best customers in a month."

The woman looked affronted. "But I've never been in here before."

"We don't give them to people who ask. They're gifts, you see."

She folded her arms over her chest. "I don't see at all. I'd like to speak to the manager."

"That would be me." LizBeth smiled.

She looked slightly taken aback, but then said, "Then bring out the owner, if you please."

"You're looking at her, too."

Just when it looked like the rude woman was about to argue, two of her friends approached. "Looks like you should have listened to us after all, Bev," one of them said. "We told you that you simply couldn't just walk in off the street and get a Daisy Bag. They're hard to get, which is why they're special."

The other woman shot LizBeth an apologetic expression. "I'm so sorry. She's usually not so demanding."

Aware that Jackson was still standing by the door, almost as if he were ready to run forward and save her from the rude woman, LizBeth simply shrugged. "I've learned that we all don't necessarily get what we want. Perhaps she's learning that now, too."

Jackson's eyes widened as the women chuckled again. Then, with a small salute, he turned around and walked out.

Through the large front window of the store, Lizbeth watched him walk to his SUV. It was a small thing, but maybe he was taking another look at her. Maybe even realizing that she was a lot of things, but most of all she wasn't a shrinking violet who fell apart at the smallest crisis.

"Would you help me find a cast-iron frying pan?" a woman asked as she approached the counter.

"But of course. That's why I'm here."

Five hours later, she was at her apartment, looking in the mirror and wondering why in the world she'd decided to buy a new outfit on the way home from work.

It wasn't a fancy dress or anything. Just a cute long printed skirt with a light blue T-shirt. But, with her favorite jean jacket over the T-shirt and her hair falling in soft waves around her shoulders, she thought she looked pretty good—and quite a bit different from how she looked in her work clothes. It was certainly far different from how she'd looked when they were dating.

"Oh, who are you kidding?" she told herself in the mirror. "He probably won't even notice."

But maybe that was okay. After all, getting her new purchase had certainly lifted her spirits, and putting the simple outfit together had been fun, too. And since she wasn't exactly a clotheshorse—almost the opposite— LizBeth was pretty sure it was long overdue.

"At the very least, you'll have something cute to wear on Sunday at church," she reminded herself before hurrying to grab her purse and make sure her small living room was picked up.

But when she looked around, everything was in order, just as it should be. And she still had fifteen minutes before he was to arrive.

Needing a shot of encouragement, she picked up her phone and called Aunt Cassie.

Cassie was Mennonite, and belonged to an even more liberal and progressive church than LizBeth. Cassie drove, had a computer, a cell phone and even a fifty-five-inch big-screen television. Most people who met her would never imagine that she was Mennonite.

But those who knew her realized her faith was strong and she was a wealth of information and comfort.

She answered on the first ring.

"What's going on, LizBeth? I thought you were going out with Jackson Lapp tonight."

"I am. I'm just ready a little early."

"Ah, and you're feeling at your wit's end."

"Something like that."

"Want to tell me what you're thinking?"

"I'm thinking I bought a new outfit, that I'm excited for Jackson to see it and that he probably only wants to grill me about possible suspects for his case."

"Truly?" She chuckled. "That sounds a bit much, Liz."

She supposed Cassie had a point. "Okay, maybe it won't quite be that bad, but I keep envisioning about a dozen things going wrong."

"Or there might be a dozen things going well, right?"

"Maybe." When Cassie groaned, LizBeth sighed. "Okay, I see your point. Maybe I'm letting about a dozen fears get the best of me."

"I don't think there's any *maybe* about it."

"See? That's why I called. I need a pep talk."

"I'm thankful for the call and I'll do what I can, but honestly, I think you need to sit down and have a little chat with the Lord."

Normally, LizBeth would completely agree, but at the moment all she really wanted was to be told what to do. "Cassie, I appreciate what you're saying, but I don't know if—"

"If you haven't asked Him for His counsel, then I think you're making a foolish choice." In a gentle tone, she continued, "He already knows your worries, yes?"

Hearing that question, LizBeth nodded. "Yes. I'm sorry."

"No need to apologize. You just needed a little bit of reminding, I think," she murmured.

"I'm better now," she said. Seeing Jackson pull up, she added, "And now I better go. He's here."

"Have a good time, dear. Don't fret. Everything

will work out the way it's meant to. Everything always does."

As she walked to the door to greet Jackson, Liz-Beth sincerely hoped Aunt Cassie's words were true.

Chapter Ten

Jackson didn't date all that much. In the last two years, he'd only had a handful of dates, and none of them had been especially memorable. That had been disappointing, but he hadn't been too upset. Jackson figured it simply wasn't the right season in his life, and that the Lord wished him to wait a bit until he didn't live and breathe each of his cases.

He couldn't deny that sometimes he took his work home with him. Jackson loved working on cold cases and felt an obligation to the victim to do everything in his power to solve them and give the victim's family closure. He knew carrying that burden with him twenty-four hours a day wasn't fair to a spouse.

So he'd put his dating life on hold and concentrated on work. He often wondered if the Lord simply had other plans for him than to fall in love and get married.

But, an hour into his evening with LizBeth, Jackson began to wonder if he'd gotten everything all wrong. Maybe it wasn't that he worked too much or that the Lord had other plans for him.

Maybe the problem had been that he hadn't been dating LizBeth Troyer.

Jackson couldn't deny it—everything about his former girlfriend still appealed to him.

He liked the way she looked, and the way she approached life. He liked the way she smiled when she talked about her family. He liked the way she focused on him when he talked, as if there weren't anything else in the whole world she would've rather been doing than listening to him.

LizBeth had such a kind way about her. Somehow, she could make him feel better just by giving him a simple smile. LizBeth's optimistic outlook and positivity also helped heal the many regrets that he still carried around with him. Jackson was even starting to wonder if he had messed up both of their lives so long ago. Maybe time and distance had twisted his memories a bit.

"You sure got quiet all of a sudden," she murmured. "Are you not enjoying your meal?"

He'd taken her to the Blue Dog Bistro, which was a simple and quaint place in the center of Millersburg. It had been her recommendation, and when he'd first heard her choice, he'd been slightly taken aback. Jackson had imagined it would be stuffy and maybe catering toward folks coming in from the big cities for vacation.

Inside, though, it was filled with industrial-looking tables and chairs and had soft music and a menu filled with all kinds of sandwiches, soups, salads and simple meals, like pork chops and roast chicken. He'd loved it in an instant. The food had turned out to be just as wonderful as the decor.

But it wasn't the restaurant that had lifted his spirits.

"I'm loving my meal," he replied at last. "When you first suggested the place, I have to admit to being skeptical."

Her eyes lit up. "Were you more worried about the name or the menu?"

"A little of both, I guess. I'd been thinking of going to an Amish restaurant."

"I don't know about you, but I'm always eager for something new."

"I'm the same way." He leaned back. "This is great. I'm glad you suggested it."

She'd asked for a French dip and had eaten about two-thirds of it. Nibbling on a fry, she seemed to consider something. Though he was tempted to press her, he waited for her to gather her thoughts.

"Jackson, since we don't know each other too well anymore, I find myself second-guessing my suggestions. It's like part of me imagines that you're the same boy I used to know, and a whole other part is sure that you're a complete stranger."

"I feel the same things about you, too," he said slowly. Though he was eager to share how much he still liked her, he didn't want to scare her away.

She pushed her plate to the side. "I guess that's all normal though, *jah*? We used to know each other but a lot has happened since."

He nodded.

"Tell me more about the case."

"Now? We're supposed to be enjoying ourselves." Plus, hadn't he recently come to the conclusion that he needed to sometimes think about something besides work?

She brushed a strand of her dark hair away from her face as she leaned closer. "I appreciate that, but I'm interested, Jackson. Plus, I'm worried, too."

"What about?"

"How can it be that an Amish girl, who could have very well been in Busy's Market, is gone and no one has missed her?" She waved a hand. "Every family I know would be heartbroken and frantic with worry."

Jackson loved that she still thought every family would send out an alarm if their teenager left. Choosing his words carefully, he said, "You don't know that she hasn't been missed."

Her eyebrows rose. "Jackson, do you really think she could've left Berlin and no one around here would be talking about it?"

"We don't know for sure that she was from Berlin. Plus, some people don't talk, LizBeth."

"They might not talk about a lot of things, but they'd talk about a missing daughter or friend."

"Would they, though? My *grandmommi* wouldn't have. She would have thought that was being disrespectful." Actually, he was pretty sure his parents hadn't sent out an alarm when he left in the middle of the night.

"I suppose one never knows how other people react to grief or family troubles," LizBeth said. "I'd like to think my parents would have marched right into the sheriff's office, but I can't be sure they wouldn't have waited a bit."

"In my line of work, I've seen a lot of things. I promise you this—some folks will do anything to make sure their secrets stay hidden."

"What do you say when you have to tell them that isn't possible?"

"I say it's always better to be open and tell the truth instead of keeping secrets." Thinking about some of his past cases, Jackson added, "Nine times out of ten, I discover those secrets, anyway."

LizBeth looked taken aback. "I guess I never considered that part of your job, Jackson." Looking tentative, she added, "Do you always report what you find to other people, even if it's going to hurt the family involved?"

He nodded. "I'm usually investigating a homicide, LizBeth. The victim needs me to do whatever I can to discover the truth." Thinking about it some more, he added, "And yes, if what I find out is going to bring a killer to justice, I will report what I discover, even if it hurts the family."

LizBeth pursed her lips and looked away, which hurt. He was proud of the work he'd done. It made him sad to think she didn't view his successes in the same way he did. "My job is to work for the victims, and usually those victims are dead. I don't have the luxury to worry about hurting people's feelings."

"Even though you might be doing more harm than good?"

"You might see things differently, but I'm of the mind that one's life matters more than most anything else."

She leaned back as if struck. "I didn't mean to imply otherwise."

"Are you sure about that?"

She blinked again, then straightened, practically pulling a veil over her face. "I believe I'm done now."

"I am, too." When she simply stared at him, he added, "Would you care for dessert?"

"I would not."

He raised his hand, signaling for the check. And realized that he had just absolutely, completely messed up the night. Why had he talked about work, anyway? He was used to sidestepping questions and redirecting conversations—he did those things all the time in his job.

Why couldn't he simply enjoy dinner and conversation with a woman he found both attractive and interesting? What was wrong with him? When was he ever going to learn from his mistakes?

As Jackson silently navigated the narrow, winding road leading back to her apartment, LizBeth felt like crying. She'd ruined their evening. Instead of ignoring the case for a couple of hours like Jackson had asked her to, she'd plunged forward. And then, when she'd realized that he wasn't going to tell her something to try to make her feel better, she'd made sure he knew that she didn't like hearing what he had to say.

Like she had some kind of right to judge how he did his job.

Shifting in the passenger seat, she looked out the window. Why couldn't she have followed her own advice? That would've been so much better for both of them.

When he stopped at a light just behind a horse and buggy, Jackson chuckled to himself.

"What?"

"Oh, I was just thinking that it would've been nice to be driving a buggy right about now. And that struck me as strange. I never imagined I'd ever think that."

"Why do you wish that now?"

"I guess because then I'd be so busy worrying about the horse and the other vehicles on the road that I wouldn't have any time to think about us."

"Wait, you've been thinking about us the last ten minutes?"

As the light changed and Jackson pulled forward, he glanced her way. "Of course I have. I had high hopes for this date of ours, but instead of doing my best to charm you, I ended up being stupid."

"I don't understand why you'd think that."

"Well, maybe that's the wrong phrase but I just realized that I shouldn't have expected everything to be different after just a couple hours. No change is that easy."

"I see."

He glanced at her. "LizBeth, you know what I mean, right?"

"I couldn't begin to imagine what you mean right now."

Jackson sighed. "All I'm saying is that—" They heard a loud pop just as his SUV swerved out of control.

"What happened?" she asked as she held on to the seat while Jackson did his best to control the vehicle, all while attempting to not hit either the buggy or any other cars on the road.

At last, they came to a stop. Both of them were breathing hard. "Are you okay?" he asked.

She nodded. "Are you?" Her voice sounded hoarse and out of breath. Her hands were shaking, too.

"Yeah." He unbuckled. "I'm going to see what happened to the tire."

"I'll get out, too."

Jackson looked like he wanted to argue but didn't protest as they both exited and stood on the side of the road.

Then she saw it. The back right tire had been blown. It looked like it was little more than shreds. Jackson knelt in front of it and examined the ruined tire. As he studied it, his expression grew even more upset.

"That must have been some nail you ran over, huh?"

"I didn't run over a nail, LizBeth."

"Okay, whatever it was must have been really sharp." She peered closer at the ruined tire. "I know it's dark, but do you see anything? Maybe you ran over a jagged piece of metal or something."

"It wasn't metal." Sitting back on his haunches, he finally looked up at her. "This wasn't my fault."

"That's what guys always say," she teased. "That's why women are the better drivers. We take responsibility for ourselves."

"LizBeth."

She lifted a hand. "Not that I'm saying running over a nail was your fault."

He softened his voice. "LizBeth, honey, you're misunderstanding me. This wasn't my fault—and not because I don't want to admit to running over something."

"Then?"

"It's not my fault because someone shot at the tire."

"Shot? Like, with a gun?" She hated to sound so ditzy, but what he was saying didn't really make sense.

Jackson nodded. "Yeah. That's exactly what I'm saying. Someone wanted us to go off the road." Gazing at the horse and buggy in the distance, he frowned. "Or maybe even something worse."

LizBeth backed up and moved farther off the road. All their personal problems didn't seem so important now. "Such as?"

Getting to his feet, he turned to face her. "I think it means that you hit the nail on the head. My being here and digging around means someone is worried about their secrets getting revealed."

She felt her mouth go dry. This had to be the first time she ever regretted being right. Actually, at the moment, she wished she could have been far more wrong.

Chapter Eleven

❧

It was the first time he'd truly regretted being on the right track during a case. After inspecting the tire and relaying his fears to LizBeth, he'd moved away from her and called both Sheriff Mose Kramer and Phillip Gunther, his sergeant back in Cincinnati. He'd planned to leave a message for Phillip—the guy was hardly ever not busy—but he picked up on the second ring. "You ready to come back yet?"

As serious as the situation was, Jackson couldn't help but grin. Phillip was not only his sergeant, but a good friend. "Sorry, no," Jackson replied.

"How much more time do you think you're gonna need?"

"At least a couple more days, and it's not because I'm reconnecting with my Amish roots, Phil."

His voice turned serious. "What's going on?"

"Someone just fired a bullet at my back tire."

"Say again?"

He could practically feel Phillip gape at the phone. Jackson knew the feeling; he was having a hard time wrapping his head around what had happened himself. Briefly, he told the sergeant about the incident.

Phillip remained silent while Jackson relayed all the details. "I'm glad you weren't hurt," he said at last.

"Me, too. I'm especially glad LizBeth was okay. If something had happened to her, I don't know if I could have handled it."

"Even if she had been hurt, it wouldn't have been your fault, Lapp. You know that."

Jackson knew that was true, but somehow that didn't make it easier. After weighing his words carefully, he took a breath. "From the first moment I've gotten here, I've felt like I've been searching for a needle in a haystack, Phillip. There's a lot of history here that I haven't been a part of, and I was going on instinct alone. But now I'm wondering if maybe I landed on the right track, after all."

"Let me guess, you're not real thrilled about that."

"That's not entirely true. I mean, I'm pleased that we might crack the case for our Amish Jane Doe."

"But?" Phillip prodded.

"But you're right. I'm thinking what you're probably thinking. I'm not real fond of getting my back wheel shot out, and even less fond of putting someone I care about in danger."

"You're all alone, too. What do you need?"

Knowing the question had been coming, Jackson had been thinking about the answer. "I'm good, I think. I called the local sheriff. His name is Mose Kramer and he's a good guy."

"You might be Amish in Amish country, Lapp, but that doesn't mean you're immune to making mistakes or needing real backup. What do you know about this Mose, anyway?"

"I know he's had a lot of experience and he's former Amish like myself. He's no sleepy small-town cop, Phillip."

"If he's that good, maybe you should put him on the case and head back. He can do the legwork and give you a call if he gets a good lead."

"Sorry, but I still think I need to stay here a little longer. No one is going to confide in a stranger, and they might not even trust the sheriff. Plus, I'm still spending the majority of my time looking through lists of women who were presented with a Daisy Bag and attempting to dig a little bit deeper."

The Sergeant sighed. "Women? What about men?"

"So far, I've sorted through about a hundred names. Of those, only two of the recipients were men. That don't mean much, though," he continued, belatedly realizing he'd adopted a bit of his former way of speaking. "I mean, one of the women's male relatives or boyfriends could have taken it."

"Which brings us back to where we started," Phillip concluded with a sigh.

"Maybe. I don't know." Thinking about the upcoming meeting he had with his sister, Marie, Jackson decided he wasn't so sure. But he was in no hurry to share that.

"You've got four more days left, Lapp, then I need you back here. As much as I appreciate your interest and dedication to this cold case, there are crimes being committed in this city every day."

"I hear you, though I am due some personal time."

"You sure you want to use vacation days for a cold case?"

He knew what Phillip meant. Every officer in CPD worked too hard to not take some personal days from time to time. Everyone knew it was too easy to burn out if an officer did nothing but work. "I understand what you're saying, but I will take a couple of personal days if I have to. I'm not going to feel good about leaving just when I start to get some answers."

"But you don't have any answers yet."

"You're right. Just a busted tire."

Phillip drummed his fingers loudly enough for Jackson to hear them over the phone. "Here's the plan. You check in with me every day and in four days, if there's evidence that proves you can solve the case, we'll talk about what you do next. But if there's not, I'm going to order you back."

"You'd really deny me personal leave?"

"Let me put it this way. Sometimes people have to be saved from themselves."

He mentally rolled his eyes. "Yes, sir."

"Go get that tire fixed. Get a decent replacement, too."

"Roger that," he said before disconnecting.

Turning back to LizBeth, he saw that she was talking to an Amish couple. Everyone was speaking in Pennsylvania Dutch. All three watched him approach.

"Sorry about that," Jackson said. "I had to do some explaining to my boss about the case."

"I understood," LizBeth said. "Jackson, this is Lizzie and Merv Weaver. They moved here after you left. Lizzie and Merv, this is Jackson Lapp. He's a policeman down in Cincinnati but he's up here working on a case."

"Hi," he said as he shook Merv's hand and nodded to Lizzie. "Good to meet ya."

"Is it true that you think someone shot out your wheel?" Merv asked.

"I'm afraid so. I saw the hole. There's no doubt in my mind that it's from a bullet."

"*Mei* neighbor is *Englisch*," Merv said. "He works at a tire store. You should call him."

Lizzie smiled. "Jackson, how's that for a blessing?"

"It's a *gut* one, indeed." His first instinct had been to thank Merv but call someone else, but now he realized he was letting his pride get in the way. If he simply called an auto body shop, there was a good chance that no one would be free to come help him for hours—maybe even a day. A friend of a friend, though? Well, that was much different. "Merv, do you know the number or who we should call?"

"I do." Merv held out a hand. "I'll call him now."

Jackson passed over his cell phone. "*Danke.*"

In short order, Merv dialed the number, asked for a guy named Johnny and soon was chatting with him amiably in Pennsylvania Dutch. Jackson still knew the language, of course, but it had been so long since he'd heard it spoken so fast he had a hard time keeping up. He did understand enough, however, to realize that Johnny was going to drop everything to meet them—and bring a couple of big garbage bags for Jackson to store the parts of the tread and any other evidence they could find.

Jackson was relieved. He had a full-sized spare and could change a tire as well. But he was going to need the other man's help to change the tire quickly—and to collect any evidence that was found.

When Merv handed his cell phone back, he was grinning. "Johnny acted like he was akin to a detective on the television."

"I don't think he was that far off. He's helping us out a lot. I'm very grateful. For your help, too."

Lizzie shook off his words. "Jackson, that's what neighbors are for, ain't so?"

Jackson smiled. "Absolutely."

LizBeth beamed at them both. "Thank you both for stopping and lending a hand."

"It weren't a problem," Merv said. "Besides, I always felt bad that I could never help Charity. I hope and pray that you'll be able to help whoever you're wanting to in your case."

Jackson felt a prickle on the back of his neck. "Who's Charity?"

Merv frowned. "She was one of my sister's friends who went missing a couple of years ago."

"*Jah*, everyone said she ran off, but that weren't her way. She had a beau and a happy family," Lizzie added with a frown.

"What happened?" LizBeth asked.

"I don't know much. Except that one day she was around and the next thing everyone knew, she wasn't. *Mei shveshtah* Lilly was upset."

"You're saying Lilly never heard from her?" Jackson asked. "Are you sure?"

Merv rubbed his beard. "Lilly never did…at least, not that I'm aware of. But then, of course, it weren't like Charity's family was gonna say too much about her running off, ain't so? She shamed them, and no one likes to talk about that."

They turned and walked away while Jackson was still trying to put together everything he'd heard. Though everything inside him was screaming for Merv and Lizzie to stop and tell him more, he merely watched them walk down the street.

Beside him, LizBeth appeared to be just as shocked. Looking up at him, she whispered, "Jackson, do you think your Amish Jane Doe could be Charity?"

"I think there's a good chance. After all, the girl had to have been someone's sister and friend."

LizBeth leaned closer to him. "Wouldn't that be something if a shot tire brought you the name of your victim?"

"It would be, but stranger things have happened," he murmured. "The Lord does have His reasons for most everything."

"That is true."

Her sweet smile was beautiful. So was the way she was practically attached to his side. Unable to help himself, he wrapped an arm around her shoulders and felt a burst of satisfaction when she didn't move away.

Yes, the Lord certainly did move in mysterious ways. Why, He'd even given Jackson a case that would bring him back to Berlin…and to LizBeth's side.

Chapter Twelve

The Emersons' barn had never looked so dark or felt so ominous. As Marie continued to pace, glancing out the open barn door every two minutes, she wondered how the place had ever felt like her refuge. It currently felt like anything but.

Perhaps it had something to do with her conversation with Aaron last night. He'd acted so different from his usual easygoing self. He'd seemed fidgety and paranoid. And he'd even yelled at her when she'd told him she'd been in contact with her brother.

At first, Marie had been so confused. During their previous conversations, he'd been so patient and complimentary. He'd told her stories about how much freedom she would have once she jumped the fence and left Berlin. Aaron had even told her she was pretty and that lots of men would want to date her.

His words had felt good, even though she actually had no interest in either his compliments or the fact that strange men might find her attractive. She might be unhappy, but she was still her mother's daughter—and *Mamm* had reassured her time and again that looks were fleeting and the only relationships worth having were ones based on friendship and faith.

Though she knew some girls in her circle were a bit jealous of her looks, Marie also knew that her blond hair and blue eyes weren't her doing. They were both from the Lord.

Last night, when she'd finally told Aaron that she had no interest in dating anyone he knew, he'd gotten angry. He'd said she had no other worth except for her looks, since she wasn't smart and didn't have any skills beyond cooking and cleaning.

He'd scared her something awful. What if Aaron was right? What if she really had nothing of worth except for her looks?

When he kept pushing her to promise to leave the county with him in two days, she'd gotten so scared, she'd burst into tears and run into the woods.

Aaron had followed her. She'd actually climbed a tree and stayed motionless until long after midnight. By the time she got home, she was exhausted. She felt dirty, too. She'd wanted a shower in the worst way but hadn't dared even enter the washroom.

If she woke up her father and he saw that she wasn't in her nightgown and robe, it would have been very bad. Very bad, indeed.

"Sorry I'm so late, Marie."

She jumped. It took a second for her to recognize the voice, too. "Oh, Jackson. You scared me."

Barely glancing her way, he ran a hand through his hair. "Sorry again. I got stuck on the phone and then the bypass was closed. A semi overturned." He drew a breath, looked ready to tell her even more about his evening, but then he stopped. "Hey, what's wrong?"

Stepping closer, he murmured, "Even in the dim light I can tell you're pale. What has happened?"

She didn't know how much to say. She needed her brother—at least, the brother she'd depended on so many years ago. But trusting him came with a risk, too. What if she revealed too much and Jackson got mad at her? She didn't know if she could handle that. "I had a strange conversation with Aaron last night."

"What do you mean by strange?"

Jackson's voice had hardened. She looked away. "He… Well, Aaron acted mean and made me cry."

He stepped closer. "What did he say, Marie?"

Jackson's voice sounded harsh but his eyes were filled with compassion. She concentrated on that— he wasn't scaring her; he just sounded intense. "He… Well, he started pressuring me to promise to leave with him soon."

"When does he want you to leave town?"

"In two days' time." She held up a hand. "I told him no, though. Don't worry."

Her brother looked like he was visibly trying to control himself. He took a step backward and shook out his hands. "I see. And what did he say when you told him no?"

"He…he didn't like that much. He scared me. So I ran."

"Out into the dark?"

"Well, yeah."

"*Ach*, Marie."

His comment sounded so foreign to the man he was now. But on the other hand, it was also so very familiar. It started a giggle out of her. She hastily covered her mouth with a hand.

He almost smiled. "Hey, what did I say?"

"Nothing. It… You sounded like my *bruder* again."

"I still am. I might look different and talk different from the way I used to, but I am still your brother."

His words were sweet. So sweet, they were almost reassuring. She made herself remember that he hadn't been around for years. Brothers didn't ignore their sisters.

"So when you ran out into the night, what happened next? Did you run home?"

"*Nee*. I ran out into the woods…"

"And?"

"I climbed a tree and waited until he left."

His expression hardened. "I want to know everything about him. His description. What kind of car he drives. I'm going to go find him, Marie."

She wanted to tell him everything…but what if Jackson left again? What if she allowed herself to count on him but all he did was make promises he didn't keep and then leave without warning?

Then how would she be able to leave?

"I don't know much about him," she said at last. "I've never seen his car."

After staring at her intently for a long moment, Jackson leaned against the wall. "Marie, I'm sorry, but I think you're lying."

He was right. Of course, he was right. But if she'd learned anything over the last few years, it was that she couldn't depend on him to listen to her or to be there for her if she was in trouble. She couldn't depend on her parents, either. No, the only person she could depend on was herself.

"If you think that, it's only because we don't know

each other anymore." She held her breath, waiting for him to refute that. Waiting for him to say that while that might be true, he *wanted* to know her again. That he wanted to have a relationship with her again.

That she could trust him.

That he loved her because he was her brother.

But instead of saying any of that, Jackson folded his arms over his chest and rolled his eyes. "Come on, Marie. I'm a cop. I can spot a liar pretty easily, and that's what you are doing. Stop lying and tell me what you know about this Aaron."

And that, she supposed, was her answer. Jackson was her brother, but he was only thinking about her in relation to his case. Because that was who he was. He was a cop, not her brother.

She folded her arms across her chest as well. Mimicking his stance on purpose. Just to show Jackson that he didn't scare her one bit. "I'm sorry you think I'm lying, but there ain't anything I can do about that."

He looked incredulous. "That's all you're going to say?"

"That's all there is to say, Jackson."

"I can't believe you're working against me. That you're protecting him." His voice turned more emphatic. "Marie, this Aaron person could be a murderer. He could put you in harm's way. He could have done something terrible to you last night."

"He could also be the person to help me. He probably is."

Pure disappointment shone in his eyes. "I can't believe you're saying that."

Marie might be a whole lot younger than him. She might even be far more fragile than he ever was…but she also knew they weren't all that different in many other ways. "Believe it," she bit out. Then she turned away. She had to get out of there. Being with him felt like he was taking all the oxygen out of the room, leaving her feeling like she was gasping for breath. "See ya, Jack," she whispered as she strode to the door.

"Wait." When she kept walking, he rushed to her side. "Marie, hold on now. We should talk."

"We just did. I need to go home."

"At least let me drive you home like I wanted to last time."

Last time, she'd still believed he was going to help her out. That he cared for her. That he was going to change her life and get her out of the house.

Now she had a pretty good idea that the only thing he was going to do was use her to solve a crime and then move on.

But because saying any of that hurt, she simply picked up her pace and strode toward the woods.

"Wait!" He reached for her arm and tugged.

Though it didn't hurt, that was the last straw. "Don't touch me!"

When Jackson immediately dropped his hand and stepped back, she ran away.

It was a cowardly thing to do, but at least she was good at that. *Jah*, she was good at running away from harm.

She'd become very good at that in the last eleven years since Jackson had up and gone.

Chapter Thirteen

He had really messed up everything with his sister. Jackson had known that practically from the moment he'd said that stupid, prideful comment about being a cop. And if that hadn't proven his point, the way Marie visibly shut down in front of him cemented it.

Then there was the fact that he still hadn't been able to make things right. He was essentially banned from his house, and Marie had run away before he could apologize and make plans to see her again.

The worst part was that he had caused this recent rift. When he'd stopped listening to her, she'd stopped trusting him. It was as if one minute he'd caught a glimpse of the girl she used to be, and the next moment they were strangers again. Or maybe even worse. Marie had started acting as if she was afraid of him.

And then he'd lost her.

It had been so hard to simply stand in the doorway of that barn and watch his little sister disappear into the night, but after he'd grabbed her arm and she'd gotten so upset, he was frozen. He, more than anyone, knew how she would feel about being grabbed. He was so ashamed.

After stewing on his mistakes for half the night, he'd gone for a three-mile run early in the morning, then showered and gotten into his truck. Jackson told himself he needed to drive around town a bit, concentrate more on the case. However, the next thing he knew, he was pulling up to LizBeth's apartment with two cups of coffee.

Before he could talk himself out of it, he knocked on her door. Of course, as soon as he did that, he looked at his watch and saw it was only a little after seven in the morning. Irritated with himself for once again not thinking something through, he turned to head down the stairs.

Then the door opened.

"Jackson, what are you doing? Are you coming or going?"

Turning around, he held up the cups of coffee. "I brought you coffee, but then I realized what time it is."

To his surprise, she half smiled at him. "You certainly are the early bird, aren't you?"

"I can come back later."

"With or without fresh cups of coffee?"

Realizing that LizBeth wasn't about to turn him away, he grinned. "With whatever you want?"

"In that case, I think you'd best come on in."

Five minutes later, LizBeth, wearing gray sweatpants and a confused expression, was staring at him from across her kitchen table.

"I'm sorry I didn't call first. I hope you really were already up," he said for about the third time. And that was the truth, though he figured his words really didn't mean all that much. After all, if he'd truly been worried about disrupting her sleep, he would have never come over without calling in the first place.

"I promise, I was awake. My friend Ellen called and we caught up for a while. That's why I wasn't dressed. It wasn't because I was sleeping," she said with exaggerated patience. "Now, stop apologizing and tell me what's on your mind."

Only the amusement in her eyes kept him from apologizing again. "I couldn't sleep last night," he admitted. "I messed things up with Marie and I need to talk with someone about what to do."

She set the cup she'd been cradling between her hands on the table. "What are your options?"

"Boy, you are cutting right to the chase." For some reason, he'd kind of thought she'd utter a bunch of platitudes.

LizBeth rolled her eyes. "You're here at seven in the morning. Of course, I'm gonna get right to the point. Now, what are your choices?"

"I reckon I can either try to honor her wishes and give Marie some space and investigate this Aaron character on my own, or try to reach out to her again."

"In order to do what?"

He set his cup on the table as well. "What do you mean?"

"I feel like you have your purposes mixed up. You want to reconnect with your sister and solve your cold case."

That was exactly what he wanted to do. "Yeah, and…"

"Oh, Jackson." She sighed. "No wonder Marie was so irritated with you." She leaned forward. "Don't you get it? Marie doesn't want to be your link to solving a murder. What she wants is to be your sister again."

LizBeth was making sure she referred to Marie as his sister. He found that vaguely condescending. "I hear what you're saying, but Marie never stopped being my sister."

"I'm sorry, but I fear you are wrong."

"LizBeth, just because I haven't seen her in years, doesn't mean I haven't always considered her to be special to me. I love her."

Right before his eyes, she adopted that same militant expression she'd worn when he'd made the mistake of trying to boss her around.

"*Jah*, you love her," she said softly. "I'm not saying you don't. However, if she was still your sister, you would have kept a relationship with her. You'd be asking how you might help her. You'd be asking how she's feeling…not asking her to give you more information about a person of interest."

Jackson opened his mouth to argue, but then realized she had a point. He had said the wrong thing. No wonder Marie had acted as if he'd yelled at her. "My sister knows I care about her and how she's doing." And yes, he felt that his retort was pretty weak.

Obviously, LizBeth felt the same because she raised one eyebrow. "Is that because you've asked?"

"Yes." When LizBeth simply stared at him, he said, "I can't read her mind, you know." Before they could debate the topic further, he added, "Besides, my point is that I was stupid, she took off and I don't know how I'm going to get to see her again."

Again, LizBeth simply stared at him like he was missing the point. "What?" he asked.

"I know you are disappointed, but I do think you can try harder."

"How? She darted off in the dark."

She sipped her coffee. When she put the cup down again, she cleared her throat. "Jackson, tell me the truth. How come you are seeing me instead of Marie?"

"My parents shunned me. They're not going to welcome me back to the fold, you know."

She shook her head at him. "Who cares what they did? Go anyway."

LizBeth's words rang in his ears for hours after he'd left her apartment. To his chagrin, he found himself answering her and coming up with excuses for why it wasn't possible for him to actually go to his parents' house. But each time, one thing rang true. He could make up lots of excuses for staying away, but none of them mattered if Marie was upset with him.

He didn't really even care if his parents still shunned him. In some ways, he felt as if he was shunning them, too. But he'd stayed away long enough. No matter what happened with his job or the Amish Jane Doe case, Jackson realized that at the end of the day, he wanted to have a relationship with Marie again. He loved his sister and she needed to know that.

Family mattered. He'd forgotten that along the way, but he vowed to not forget it again.

When Jackson drove up to the house, he was startled by how much it looked the same. *Exactly* the same. The same white paint that was in need of touching up. Same flower beds meticulously cared for. The barn still looked as if it was just one strong wind away from falling down.

And there was still the same foreboding feeling of being watched. The hair on the back of his neck prickled with awareness—and the knowledge that he wasn't any more comfortable on the land than he'd been so many years ago.

Shrugging off the misgivings, he reminded himself once again about whom he was there to see. And then he got out of his truck before he changed his mind.

The front door opened when he stepped on the walkway, and his father poked his head out. His face looked haggard, and far older. His cheeks and jowls sagged, as if they were holding on for dear life to his facial bones.

"What do you want?"

Well, there was the greeting he'd both expected and dreaded. However, he wasn't a kid anymore and he certainly was no longer afraid of his father's fists. "I want to talk to Marie."

"What makes you think I would let you see her?"

"Because she is my sister."

"Jackson?"

It took a moment for Jackson to understand why his father had sounded so incredulous. And then it hit him. His father hadn't recognized him. "*Jah*," he said softly. "It's me."

His father's expression went slack before he visibly gathered himself together. He fumbled in his trousers' pockets for a pair of worn glasses. Impatiently, he put them on. "I never thought I'd see you again. I *canna* believe you came back."

"To be honest, I didn't think I ever would." When

his father continued to study him, Jackson added, "*Daed*, I'm surprised you are speaking to me."

He pursed his lips and shrugged. "You're here on my doorstep, *jah*?"

Jackson nodded.

"We never knew what happened to you. On some days, I feared the worst."

"I figured you knew. After all, you'd promised to practically keep me locked in the barn without food for days. Of course I left."

Some of the hope that had been shining in his father's eyes faded. "I don't remember any of that."

"I do. I think you do, too. You just don't want to admit it."

"What have you been doing?" He gestured toward the tan truck. "Besides jumping the fence?"

His father still hadn't opened the door more than a foot.

"Is there any way we could talk somewhere else besides the doorway?"

His father frowned, then seemed to be summoned behind him. Jackson heard the low murmur of his mother's voice. So quiet and tentative. So familiar. Moments later, the door opened and Jackson got his first real look at both of his parents.

His father was still skeletally thin, his mother still slim and nervous-looking. That was the same.

The differences, however, were many. Their hair had turned white. They seemed to have shrunk in size. But, surprisingly, the most shocking difference was the way they were standing together.

It now seemed that they were leaning on each other for support instead of his father standing alone.

"Jackson," his mother murmured. "*Wilcom*. Come inside."

When they both moved to one side, he did as they asked…wondering all the while if being invited inside was a blessing or a terrible mistake.

He supposed that only God—and time—would tell.

Chapter Fourteen

The first thing Jackson noticed about the house was that the floors were exactly like he remembered. They were well cared for and smelled like lemon oil. The rooms were still dark, despair continued to permeate the air and there were so many pieces of furniture crammed into each room that he felt claustrophobic.

It felt like home.

From the time she'd decided to acknowledge him, his mother had become a nervous, fluttery bird. "Want to come to the kitchen?" she asked as she led the way down the hall. "I could make us some coffee. Or tea, if you prefer that now." She stopped and turned to him. "Do you drink tea now?"

"*Nee, Mamm*. I still drink *kaffi*, and that sounds *gut. Danke.*"

She smiled tentatively before turning back toward the kitchen.

Jackson watched her for a moment, struggling to figure out what looked different about her. It took him a second but he realized what was going on with her gait. It was uneven. "What happened to you?"

She paused but didn't turn back around. "Why nothing, of course."

"*Mamm*, I see how you're walking. You've got a limp."

"Hush now. Don't worry. I am okay."

But when he saw that same uneven gait again, he flinched, both at her lies and the ball of guilt that was forming in his stomach. "Did my father hurt you?"

She rested a hand on the spotless kitchen counter. "Do not worry about me. I am all right."

This conversation was familiar, too. He'd grown up learning to pretend his backside wasn't hurting. That he didn't have a bruise on his arm. That his mother's eyes weren't filled with pain. That was his legacy, he supposed. He'd learned how to lie well from his parents. It was a handy tool when conducting police investigations. In life? Not so much.

"Mother, I have a right to know what happened."

Her expression hardened. "You've been gone for a dozen years. I don't think you have that right at all." When he tried to interrupt, she shook her head. "Jackson, forgive me, but I don't wish to discuss it."

He gritted his teeth but held his tongue. She was right, he had been gone too long. "Like I said, coffee does sound good." It was an inane thing to say but at least it filled the strained silence in the air.

His mother's shoulders eased as she opened up a cupboard and took out four cups. Jackson watched her for a moment.

"Where is the *kaffi*, Myra?" his father asked as he entered the room.

His father's demanding voice spurred a burst of anger that he couldn't hold back. "*Mamm* has a limp. What did you do to her, *Daed*?"

His father's eyes widened but he answered readily enough. "It was an accident."

"What happened?"

He waved a hand. "I lost my temper, shoved her out of the way on the landing upstairs and she fell down." His tone was so very matter-of-fact. Almost like he was describing the weather.

Jackson gaped at him. He couldn't remember a time when his father had ever admitted to doing anything wrong, let alone taken responsibility for another's pain. Was this progress? He truly had no idea.

His mother shrugged. "My leg never quite healed because I refused surgery. But, as I told you, Jackson, it ain't none of your concern."

"Why would you refuse surgery?"

"You know how costly surgeries are."

Trying hard to push aside the mixture of emotions spinning inside him—the guilt that he'd never known about the accident, the overwhelming anger he felt toward his father, since he was responsible for the injury in the first place—he realized he was helpless to make anything better. He took a deep breath and tried to focus on them instead of himself. "What about the church? They have collections for that."

His mother only stared at him like he was a *dumm Englischer* who had a lot to learn about Amish life. Or maybe simply about life.

"If we took that much money, we would be beholden," she said.

"Since you didn't get surgery, you are lame, *Mamm*."

"It's a little late to worry about her, ain't so?" *Daed* asked. "You've been gone a long time."

"I never stopped worrying."

"You have a poor way of showing it, then. We haven't heard from you in years." His father took the cup of coffee *Mamm* held out.

"I had no choice but to leave. Besides, I was fairly sure I was shunned." Turning to his mother when she held out a cup to him, Jackson added, "I know you recognized me at Busy's, *Mamm*. Yet you walked past me as if I didn't exist."

"You know I had no choice."

He did know that. Only his father's decision to acknowledge him would enable his mother to change.

Why was he arguing about all of this, anyway? It wasn't like his parents had made the rules. They came from generations of traditions combined with a belief in their ways—and what was best for the continuation of their way of life. Those rules had served the community well for a very long time.

"May I speak to Marie?"

His father sat down in one of the chairs at the kitchen table. "Why?"

"I cannot tell you."

"Why not? Because it involves your police business?" *Daed* asked.

That caught him off guard. "I didn't know you knew I'd become a cop."

"People talk. At times I listen."

Jackson didn't know whether to laugh or roll his eyes. But then he caught his mother's eyes—and saw amusement there. She knew her husband was being stubborn and silly. She was not oblivious to his faults.

"I need to speak to Marie about a case I am working on."

His father took a long sip of coffee before replying. "There is no need for her to be involved in the outside world."

"I'm afraid there is a need. A young Amish woman who I am fairly sure was from this area was found in downtown Cincinnati. She was lured away."

"What do you mean by found?" *Mamm* asked as she joined them at the table. "Was she hurt?"

"She was killed, *Mamm*."

She gasped. "Our Marie is not involved in anything of that nature. She is a good girl."

"I agree. But she might know something that can help." When both of his parents looked like they were about to argue further, Jackson blurted, "I have to ask her questions. The girl who died might have left on her own, might have been taken…might have even been shunned, I don't know. All that matters is that whoever did this needs to be found before they hurt another woman."

Of course, it went without saying that since the death was a cold case, the perpetrator could very well have hurt many other women in the two years since the case had grown cold.

But his parents didn't need to know about that.

Some of the distrust that had been so present in his father's expression faded as concern filled his gaze. Turning to Jackson's mother, he inclined his head slightly.

"She isn't here," *Mamm* said at last.

His whole body went on alert. "What do you mean? Is she missing?" What if someone had taken her last night when he had let her go instead of chasing after her? If that had happened, it was all his fault.

"Oh, my stars, *nee*! Marie ain't missing at all,"

Mamm said. "We allowed her to go to a quilting this morning."

Relief filled him. As he struggled to regain his composure, he leaned back and linked his fingers on the top of the table. "Ah. Do you know when she'll return?"

"Likely not for a few hours."

"But you might remember the friend she went to go see," his father murmured. "Her name is LizBeth Troyer. Does her name ring a bell?"

Yes, there was definitely a glint of humor in his father's eyes now.

"You know it does."

His mother smiled. "It's none of my business, of course, but you might want to pay LizBeth a visit as well. She never married...but perhaps you already know that, too?"

Jackson might have left home years ago, and he might have proven himself in the line of duty more than once. But it seemed that no matter what happened in his life, there were still times when he was only his parents' son...and he felt at a disadvantage yet again.

Chapter Fifteen

LizBeth was still wearing her flannel pajamas when Marie knocked on the door. Honestly, she probably wouldn't have even heard the timid-sounding knock if she hadn't been attempting to keep her philodendron alive by giving it another drink of water.

Even then, she probably would've still ignored the knock, except she'd been afraid that weak knock had come from Mrs. Krentz two doors down. Sometimes her elderly neighbor knocked on random doors when she needed help at home.

But when LizBeth had peeked through the peephole and saw Marie, it hadn't occurred to her to do anything else but free the dead bolt and immediately let the younger girl in.

"Hiya, Marie."

"H-oh! I woke you up. I'm sorry."

"You didn't wake me up at all. It's my day off from work and I'm afraid I'm being lazy." She smiled and gestured for her to come in. "Your visit is a wonderful, *gut* surprise."

Marie still didn't smile, though she did walk inside

and close the door behind her. Her eyes widened as she looked around the space. LizBeth wondered if Marie was more shocked by the small space or the fact that she had a flat-screen television anchored on her wall.

"Is this your very own apartment?"

"If you mean do I live here by myself, yes, it's just me. It's not very big, but one can only be in one room at a time, right?"

"That is true, I suppose."

"Would you like something to drink? I have *kaffi*. Or iced tea and some soda, too."

"What kind of soda?"

"Orange soda in glass bottles." LizBeth grinned, almost like she was offering something slightly scandalous. She might have been *Englisch* for many years, but she'd never lost her appreciation for a cold soda. Growing up, it had been such a rare treat.

"Oh, I'll have that," Marie said with a smile. "*Danke.*"

Feeling like she'd made great strides, though she had no idea about what, LizBeth pulled out two bottles from the refrigerator and opened them. Then, deciding they would both probably be more comfortable sitting at her small dinette than on her loveseat, she placed them in front of the two chairs and sat down in one of them.

Marie studied her, studied the soda and then joined her. LizBeth stayed quiet, merely took a sip of her soda and sighed in appreciation. It really was so good—even first thing in the morning.

After Marie took a sip as well, she grinned. "This is tasty."

"Right? I'm glad you like it, too."

Marie took another sip, then folded her hands primly

on the table in front of her. "I suppose you must be wondering why I'm here."

"I'm mainly wondering how you got here. You didn't walk, did you?"

"*Nee*. I have a little bit of money. I used it to hire a driver."

"I'm sorry you had to do that." LizBeth knew that Marie's parents would never give her spending money, and they carefully managed everything she might have made selling flowers or vegetables on a roadside stand near the house.

"I didn't have much choice." Setting the soda down, she added, "You see, I'm confused. I needed to talk to someone who still knows Jackson."

Which, as far as LizBeth knew, was only her. "Why? What has happened?"

"I saw him last night. At the Emersons' barn."

"Your parents allowed that?"

"Oh, *nee*," she said in a more confident tone. "It was late at night. It was the second time we met together."

"I'm sure it's nice to see him again."

Looking stricken, Marie looked down at her lap. "I don't know if that's how I feel."

She and Jackson might still be figuring things out, but she was absolutely sure that he adored Marie and wanted to get to know her again. "Why is that?"

"How did you feel, seeing him? Or have you been seeing him all this time?"

"I hadn't seen him in twelve years. Not until the day you and I first saw him at the market." Taking another sip of soda, LizBeth allowed herself to think about Marie's question. She'd felt so many things when she'd first spied Jackson, it was hard to put into words. "I felt a lot of things when we first spoke, I guess. Relief that he was still alive…followed by confusion about why he had returned, followed by anger that he'd been gone all this time but seemed able to saunter right back into my life, almost as if nothing had happened." She laughed softly. "I guess all that means I feel a lot of things whenever I'm around him." Of course, she also felt giddy and infatuated, but she wasn't going to share that! "What about you?"

"I felt many of the same things. But now? Well, now he wants my help." She pursed her lips like she'd just bit into a lemon. "Maybe he only wants my help for his case. Not to get to know me again."

"I know how you're feeling, Marie, but I promise, Jackson really does still love you and wants to be a part of your life again. He's told me so."

Hope filled her blue eyes before she blinked it away. "And what else is going on with him?"

"He's also trying to solve a murder." Seeing how pensive Marie still looked, LizBeth added, "Are you afraid to help him?"

"I might be."

"Why? And I'm asking honestly, not in a mean way."

"I don't want my parents to find out, of course. But that isn't the main reason. The main one is… I'm afraid to trust Jackson again. What if I risk a lot to help him and he just leaves again?"

"He *is* going to leave again, Marie. His home is in Cincinnati."

She bit her lip. "So I shouldn't help him or trust him?"

"No, I think you should, because even though Jackson is going to eventually return to Cincinnati, I don't think he's going to stay away from Berlin anymore."

"So what? He'll come back in another five years?"

Marie's tone was bitter. It was obvious she was harboring so much heartache and pain.

"No, I think he's missed being here. And you," she added with a small smile. Who knew? Maybe Jackson was hoping to see more of her, too…but LizBeth wasn't quite ready to count on that.

"If he cares so much about me, why did he stay away?"

"You know why."

"Because of what happened between you and him. Because your parents shunned you as well."

"*Nee!*" LizBeth was genuinely shocked. "No, that wasn't how it was at all. Did you really think that's why Jackson left?"

"That's what my parents told me happened."

"I don't know why, but they lied to you, Marie. Yes, my parents were upset with me, but they didn't punish me severely. All I really got was a lecture. Later, when I explained how I never really felt comfortable living Plain and didn't think I would ever completely embrace the way of life, they listened."

"They didn't get mad?"

"I'm not going to say that they weren't disappointed, but they understood." She paused, remembering that conversation like it had happened only the day before. "My father eventually shared that he wasn't surprised by my choice. He said he'd always known I was interested in the outside world." She took a deep breath. "It was nothing like what happened to Jackson."

Marie took a deep breath. "They were awful to him. My parents used to be so much worse."

"I'm glad they're more lenient now."

"Things aren't as bad as when Jackson was home, but they are far from lenient. I canna wait to leave."

LizBeth reached for her hand. "You know you aren't alone, right? Not only will God help you during this time, I am sure Jackson will do whatever it takes to help you. I will, too."

"*Danke*, but I already told my *bruder* that I didn't need his assistance. Someone else has offered to help me, you see."

LizBeth didn't see what Marie meant at all. What Marie was about to do wasn't easy. The Amish way of life was a peaceful and faithful one. It was also governed by rules and restrictions. If one wasn't used to a lot of freedoms or the rules and regulations in the outside world, that was confusing and difficult, too. Even she had had a difficult time adjusting, and she hadn't been baptized and had a supportive family.

"You've been baptized, yes?"

"Of course." Sounding bitter again, she tossed her head hard enough for the strings of her *kapp* to flutter around her neck. "Do you think my parents would have allowed me to do anything else?"

"Are you worried about your promises to God?"

"My promises to Him are personal ones. He knows I didn't have a choice."

"But still…it might be hard." That was putting it mildly, too. Getting baptized in the Amish faith was very serious. Breaking that covenant was akin to getting divorced—and that wasn't allowed, either.

"Who do you know that is going to help you?"

"It's a man who has helped a lot of other Amish girls leave."

"Do you trust him?"

"Of course I do. I mean, why wouldn't I?"

"Well, a lot of people say things without meaning them, you know."

"I know that. I'm not a child."

But that was the problem, LizBeth thought. Marie kind of *was* just a child. She was a very sheltered, very naive-in-the-ways-of-the-world Amish woman. Taking another tack, she said, "Do you know of any women this man has helped?"

"I think so."

"All right. What happened to them after they left, Marie? Where did they go?"

Dismay filled her expression before she tamped it down. "You know I can't go visit any of those girls. My parents barely let me come over here, and I told them I was helping you with a quilt."

"All I'm asking is where they are living now. Do you know that? Are the girls this man helped all resettled in the same place?"

"I don't know that answer."

"You need to figure that out, Marie. The *Englisch* world offers a great many choices. Some are good, but others are far more dangerous." LizBeth knew she sounded vague, but she was reluctant to say anything too awful. She didn't want to scare Marie, just make sure she understood that things were very different from Berlin. "Once you leave your home, if you don't have a good support system, a lot of trouble can come find you."

"I'll be fine. You are worrying too much."

LizBeth was beginning to feel frustrated. Oh, but this girl was so foolish—and full of herself, too! It was a dangerous combination. "If you don't know where you're going to live, what are you going to do to support yourself?"

Marie's confident expression turned slack. "What do you mean?"

"Life costs money. Even my little apartment costs almost a thousand dollars a month to rent. How are you going to pay for your food and housing? What are you going to do for work?"

"Aaron said I don't need to worry about such things." But she looked a lot more unsure.

At least she had a name now. Aaron wasn't much help—there were a lot of Amish and former-Amish men by that name. A lot of others named that who had nothing to do with their community as well.

"Marie, are you really telling me that you are willing to put your whole future in a stranger's hands without asking any questions?"

"It's not like that." Looking more agitated, she added, "Besides, you aren't listening. I came over to talk to you about Jackson. Not Aaron."

"You're right, you did. And to finally answer your question, yes, I think you can trust Jackson and depend on him, too."

"You sound so sure."

"I am. Jackson has been gone a long time and he might be a policeman now, too. But in his heart, he's still the same man. I know he still loves you, too."

"Maybe—but is love even enough to overcome ev-erything that's happened? I just don't know."

Her mouth suddenly dry, LizBeth took a final swig of her orange soda. For the first time since they'd started talking, she didn't have an answer for Marie.

Huh. Maybe Marie wasn't so foolish, after all.

Chapter Sixteen

Marie had been foolish when she'd lied to her parents, hired a driver and knocked on LizBeth's apartment door without receiving an invitation first. Oh, she hadn't felt that way at the time. Instead, she'd felt so confident and mature. And grown up! After all, she'd asked around and gotten LizBeth's address on her own. Then she'd used most of her savings and hired a driver to get there, which she'd never done before.

It had taken a lot of gumption to walk up the stairs to LizBeth's apartment and knock on the door, too. As it had to share the purpose of her visit. But even then, she'd been full of hope and pride.

However, she'd soon learned how stupid she had been to have such high hopes for her meeting with LizBeth.

Yes, that meeting had been a true disappointment. Instead of focusing on Jackson and the stranger he'd become, LizBeth had dwelled on Marie's choices and her decisions. No matter how many times she'd told LizBeth that she knew what she was doing, LizBeth had asked her questions and acted as if she didn't have a single smart hair on her head.

She'd kept asking about Aaron, too—as if Marie hadn't been smart enough to keep a secret.

It had been tempting to answer LizBeth's questions, just to see her expression when she learned how crafty and smart Marie had been. She'd wanted to tell Liz-Beth just how good he was. After all, she'd talked with Aaron after he'd scared her. He'd apologized, saying he just wanted to help her and he got frustrated. She knew he was sorry for scaring her—he was a good man. Just how wonderful could her life be, if she gave him a chance?

But Marie hadn't dared break her promise to Aaron. He'd already warned her that if she broke their code of silence, he'd never even help her make a phone call. She knew he'd been completely serious, too.

So instead, all Marie had been able to do was evade LizBeth's nosy questions.

Well, now she sure had a lot of time to think about things, since she had to walk home. She hadn't thought about how much it would cost to hire a driver to get home. No, she'd actually thought that LizBeth would've driven her home.

She probably would've, too…if Marie hadn't left in such a hurry.

Seeing that she was near the orchard, she picked up her pace. At this rate, she wasn't going to get home for another hour. Maybe more. She'd get in trouble for that. Chewing on her bottom lip, she tried to come up with a story that her parents might believe. Hmm. Maybe LizBeth had a sick pet so she couldn't take her home?

Would they ever believe such a thing?

"Marie?"

Startled, she turned, and then peered inside the car that had just pulled up next to her. "Aaron? Oh, my word! What are you doing here?"

"I could ask you the same thing," he said with one of his trademark smiles that never failed to make her heart melt a little bit. "What in the world are you doing, walking on the side of the road like this?"

"I'm walking home. I was at a friend's house."

"Really?" He looked behind her. "Is she with you?"

"No. I'm alone."

"Marie, you can't walk home all alone. Why, anyone driving by might accidentally hit you. We both know that's not safe." He motioned toward the passenger-side door. "Get in."

Aaron was so kind, and she supposed he did have a point, even though she hadn't really been afraid of vehicles hitting her. No, she'd only been thinking about how she was going to arrive home late and wet from the drizzling rain without getting in trouble.

But still, she hesitated. Before now, she'd only spoken to him at night when there was hardly anyone else around. What if someone outside her circle found out and told her parents?

A car honked as it veered around Aaron's vehicle. "I can't stay here much longer, Marie," he said. "I'm liable to cause a wreck if I do. I'd hate that, and I'd hate if it happened because you didn't trust me."

"I would hate that, too." She took a step closer but didn't grasp the handle.

"You do trust me, don't you?"

"Of course." After all, hadn't she just admitted to LizBeth that she couldn't trust Jackson?

"Well, then, come on." He leaned farther over and opened the passenger-side door. "Stop stalling. Come on in before we cause a wreck."

He was so sure. So friendly. Plus, what was she worried about, anyway? It wasn't like there were a bunch of her parents' friends walking on the side of the road. No one would ever find out that she was with him.

"All right." She smiled up at him "Thank you for stopping."

"I'm really glad I did," he said as he drove back onto the road. "Put your seat belt on, okay?"

She buckled up as he sped down the road. It started to rain harder. "If you hadn't shown up, I would have been pretty soaked right about now." Wiping off a few stray raindrops, she added, "Your timing was perfect."

"I feel the same way. Obviously, the Lord was looking out for both of us, right?"

"Right." She didn't actually want to bring the Lord into the conversation. That didn't feel right at all.

Looking more satisfied, Aaron grinned as he switched lanes. "What were you doing out here on your own, anyway?"

"I wanted to speak to a friend. I went to her house for a while."

"Really? Is she in your church district?"

"*Nee.* She is just a woman I know through my brother."

Aaron frowned. "I thought your brother jumped the fence."

"He did. He, um, just happens to be back here on a case."

Stopping at the light, he looked at her intently. "What kind of case is that?"

"Oh, well, it's a police case. He's a policeman."

"Your brother is a cop."

She smiled slightly. "It's hard to believe, right?"

"I don't recall you ever telling me that he was a cop here on a case. Why didn't you?"

"There wasn't much reason to. I didn't know he was a cop. I hadn't seen Jackson in years."

"Why not?"

"He left when he was about my age." Feeling uncomfortable with both the intense way Aaron kept staring at her and the questions, she glanced out the passenger-side window. Nothing looked familiar. "Uh-oh. I think we were supposed to turn already. You might have missed my street."

"Don't worry. I'll turn around soon."

But he was still in the left-hand lane. Still driving very fast. "When?"

"Whenever I can." He glanced at her again, giving her a condescending smile. "Don't worry. I've got you."

Marie smiled back at him, but she knew it was tentative at best. The truth was that her insides were starting to knot and she was beginning to feel like maybe Aaron wasn't exactly as sweet and comforting as she'd thought he was.

"Tell me more about your brother, Marie. His name is Jackson, you said?"

"*Jah.* I mean, yes. His name is Jackson Lapp."

"Where does he live? Mansfield or Columbus?"

"*Nee.* In Cincinnati." Marie clenched her hands on her lap. Her voice was starting to quiver.

Aaron's voice turned hard. "He's a long way from home, isn't he? What brought him to Berlin? Was it really a police case, or did you ask him to come here?"

She squirmed uncomfortably. She was starting to wish she could just hop out of the car, but there was no chance of doing that. Even with the rain pouring down, Aaron was practically racing down the road. "Jackson is investigating the murder of an Amish girl who he thinks was from here."

"Really? Which Amish girl?"

"Which?" That seemed like an odd way of phrasing it.

"Her name, Marie. What was her name?"

"Um, he doesn't know her name. She, um, died a while back. Two years ago."

Aaron relaxed slightly. "He must be a really good policeman if he followed the trail all the way here, hmm?"

"I don't know. I don't know much about his job." As they passed another exit, she said, "I really want to go home now. My parents are gonna be worried. Will you turn around?"

"I will. Just not yet," he said.

"But—"

"Stop telling me what to do, Marie." His voice had turned hard. "I promise, it will be better if you learn to do as I say and not ask questions. It will be much easier for you."

Marie didn't know what he meant by that, but she was afraid she was about to find out.

And she wasn't only afraid of that. She was afraid in general. Just very, very afraid.

Chapter Seventeen

Jackson had ended up spending the day with his parents. After the first awkward hour, the three of them had seemed to come to an unspoken agreement. They wouldn't talk about the past. Instead, they focused on the present—and on chores that needed to be done.

After his mother made them a warm lunch of soup and sandwiches, he'd asked if he could help take care of some tasks his father had been having a difficult time doing on his own.

Slipping into the ease of the moment, his father agreed. Next thing Jackson knew, he was repairing a back step. Soon after, he and his father were fixing a leaky faucet in the bathroom.

As they steadily worked side by side, Jackson felt some of the pain and anger he'd been harboring for so long dissipate. His father seemed to feel the same way, because his words and directions slowly became less stilted and more conversational. Eventually, to Jackson's surprise, his father even began to ask him questions about his job. He would've never guessed it, but it seemed that his father enjoyed mysteries and detective stories.

As the hours passed, each one of them started to glance out the window more frequently. Marie's absence was noted, and it was obvious they all felt like she should've been home far earlier.

Jackson was also pleased to notice that his father seemed more concerned than angry that Marie was late. He would have never imagined his *daed* choosing that path, but he was glad of it. Maybe the Lord really had been working with his father and was helping him become a better person. He sure hoped so.

By the time the sun had started to dip over the horizon, none of them could deny what was going on. Marie was very late and it wasn't like her. Not at all.

After glancing at his watch for what felt like the thirtieth time, he said, "Where do you think she could be?"

His parents exchanged solemn, worried glances. "I couldn't begin to guess," *Daed* said. "She was going to see LizBeth like we told *ya*, but it was just to work on a quilt."

"A quilt?"

His mother shrugged. "I didn't believe LizBeth was much of a quilter but I allowed her to go, anyway. Marie's been so restless of late. I thought she might learn something from an older woman." She glanced out the window again. "But she should have been home by now."

"It's five o'clock. It's raining and getting dark." He was well aware they could see the same thing he could, but he felt like he needed to emphasize that.

Walking to one of the front windows, *Manm* peered out. "Maybe Marie decided to stay with LizBeth."

He'd already tried her cell phone once. LizBeth hadn't answered. He hadn't wanted to leave a text— he wasn't sure if he was being ridiculous or simply cautious. But now he was getting antsy. In addition, he was starting to get a feeling that something was very wrong.

"I'll try calling LizBeth. She should be done with work now, if she went to the store after Marie's visit."

Looking relieved, his mother nodded. "Or perhaps Marie went with her. She loves looking around Busy's."

This time, instead of walking outside, Jackson called LizBeth from the living room so his parents wouldn't have to wait for news.

She answered on the second ring. "Jackson, hey! Sorry I didn't pick up last time you called. I ended up going into the store. It's been busy."

"You're at the store now?"

"Yes." Sounding confused, she added, "My cousin Harlan opened for me, but then I've been here with Fern most of the day. Why? Do you need something?"

"No, but I was wondering if maybe Marie was with you?"

"No. She left my house hours ago."

Feeling like the wind had just been taken from his sails, Jackson sank down on the chair. It was a struggle not to panic, but he'd learned doing his investigative work that panicking and jumping to conclusions never helped anyone—and most especially not the person who was in trouble.

"Where could she have gone after seeing you? Any idea?"

"I'm sorry, but I have no idea at all." After a pause,

LizBeth added, "I'm afraid Marie got upset with me and kind of left in a hurry. I had meant to take her home but I was still in my pajamas. By the time I thought to look for her, she was long gone."

"So you didn't take her home," he murmured, mainly for his parents' benefit.

"I promise, I intended to drive her, but Marie acted like she couldn't get out of my apartment fast enough." She paused. "Her showing up at my door caught me off guard, Jackson. I didn't know she was going to come over."

"You didn't make plans with her?"

"*Nee*," she answered, sounding defensive. "Now, what is going on? Why are you asking me all these questions?"

"I'm at my parents' *haus*." Looking at both his parents, he added, "I took your advice and came over here. We've had a nice visit. But Marie hasn't come home."

"Really? Oh, no. Is there any chance she could've gone to a friend's house or something?"

"My parents don't think so. I'll check but it's doubtful."

"Oh, poor Marie. It's been raining for hours. Maybe she stopped somewhere to wait it out."

"Yeah. Maybe so." But Jackson didn't need to see LizBeth's face to know that neither of them thought that was a real possibility. Marie wouldn't risk her father's wrath and just not show up. He might not know his sister real well anymore, but he certainly knew that.

"What can I do to help?"

Jackson glanced at his parents. Both looked shaken and worried, older and frailer than they had even that morning. To his surprise, he wasn't quite ready to leave them yet. "If you see or hear from her, let me know. Otherwise, I'll be in touch."

"Please call or text when you see her, Jackson. You've got me worried now."

"Will do. Thanks."

"What did she say, Jack?" his father asked. "Did she have any news?"

He tried to think of the best way to convey the conversation to them. But bad news was bad news…and the truth couldn't be disregarded. Not ever.

Bracing himself, he crossed the room to face them. "LizBeth said that Marie left her apartment hours ago."

"She didn't take her anywhere?" *Mamm* asked.

"No." He sighed, trying to imagine what had happened between LizBeth and his sister. "I don't know what exactly was said between the two of them, but Marie got mad and wouldn't let LizBeth drive her home. She ran out of the apartment before LizBeth had a chance to offer a ride."

"What do you mean by had a chance?" *Mamm* asked. "LizBeth shouldn't have let her leave!"

"*Mamm*, I don't know Marie too well anymore, but even I know that she wouldn't have allowed LizBeth to order her around. Marie is headstrong."

"She is," *Mamm* said. "She didn't used to be, but she's been restless ever since she graduated eighth grade." Her gaze flickered to his father but she didn't add anything else.

Jackson remembered some of the comments Marie had made. Their father might be a calmer version of his former self, but he wasn't a completely different man. He'd hurt Marie, and she hadn't wanted to be hurt again.

"I'm going to wait here with you two for another

half hour. Then, if we still don't see her, I'm going to go out looking for her."

"It will be dark and she could be anywhere," *Daed* said. "Anywhere at all."

"I know. LizBeth guessed that Marie might have stopped somewhere to get out of the rain."

His mother brightened. "I can see her doing that. She wouldn't like to be caught in the rain."

His shoulders easing slightly, Jackson's father nodded. "She never did like getting wet. I bet that's what she's doing. Taking a rest before walking the rest of the way home. I'm sure of it."

Jackson didn't know if his parents believed those words any more than he did. But maybe it didn't even matter. He learned over the years that hope was a powerful thing. Without hope or faith, a person had very little to keep them going.

He hoped he was wrong but it sure felt like they were about to need all the hope—and faith—they could possibly gather.

Two hours later, he pulled into LizBeth's apartment complex and stared up into her window. The lights were on, which he took to be a sign that she was home. He really hoped so. He'd spent the last ninety minutes driving down the highway while looking for signs of his sister.

As Jackson had feared, he hadn't seen a thing. But his backward path had brought him to LizBeth's place, and even if she didn't have any news, Jackson knew he needed to see her. He felt alone and discouraged and helpless. Three things he hadn't felt since the moment he'd left home with a couple of broken ribs and only a strong will to sustain him.

"Jackson!" she said the moment she answered the door. "I'm so glad to see you."

Maybe it was her smile, or the warm glow of her apartment, or just because he was scared to death, but he pulled her into his arms and held her close.

She buried her nose in his neck and wrapped her arms around him, holding on tight. Feeling her soft body, inhaling the sweet scent of her honey-infused shampoo, Jackson exhaled in relief. He was scared to death about Marie, he was confused about his relationship with his parents, and he was torn up with guilt that he might have somehow caused his sister to take off. But at least he wasn't alone.

Not anymore.

Chapter Eighteen

Feeling Jackson's shudder, LizBeth rubbed his back, even though she feared that her light, tentative touch didn't do much good. She felt so small next to him.

But after another two minutes passed and he was still holding her in his arms, LizBeth started to get even more worried. She'd never known Jackson Lapp to ever act so insecure or upset. Honestly, the only time she'd ever seen him out of control and at a loss as to what to do was the moment her brother had caught them at that party.

But that had certainly been the exception. The Jackson she'd grown up with had been confident and rock solid. Jackson had been the type of boy to never be flustered or troubled. When they'd been young teenagers in school, he'd been the boy everyone looked up to. He seemed to have all the answers, always got along with the teacher and took everything in with ease.

Now that he was an *Englischer* police officer, she'd seen that same confidence shine through. So much that at first she'd resented how easily he had seemed to adapt to seeing her again.

Even her initial cool welcome hadn't seemed to faze him.

Feeling useless, she patted him on the back again. "Jackson, what do you need?"

Whether it was the question, or that he'd finally gotten control of his emotions, he stepped away. "Sorry, LizBeth. I, uh, didn't meant to latch on to you like a starfish."

She smiled at his phrasing. "It was just a hug, Jackson. We certainly have hugged before, *jah*?"

His cheeks flushed. "*Jah.* Of course." He swiped at a wayward strand of hair that had fallen into his eyes. "I don't know what's wrong with me." He closed his eyes. "Scratch that. I do know. I'm just on edge."

"What is wrong? Are you worried because you still haven't heard from Marie?"

"Yes, but that isn't all of it." He shook his head. "My parents are upset and I'm trying to keep hold of myself…but I just don't know, LizBeth. I'm starting to really worry about her."

"What can I do?"

"Tell me what you two talked about. As much as you remember." Before she could gather her thoughts, he added, "You said she left in a hurry?"

LizBeth forced herself to calm down and think. "She did. I'm afraid she was frustrated with me. I think she came here looking for some answers and I didn't have many to give."

"What kind of answers was she looking for?"

"Well, she was mainly concerned about, Jackson."

"Me?" He looked completely taken aback.

"Of course you, Jackson. Marie loves you. She kept asking if I thought she could trust you."

He looked crushed. "Boy, I really messed up with her, didn't I?" He swallowed hard. "I hope you told her that she could trust me."

"I did. Of course, I told her to trust you." That was easy to share. Everything else? Well, that wasn't going to be as easy.

Practically reading her mind, he murmured, "Why am I getting the feeling that there's more to the story?"

"Probably because there is." She hesitated. Jackson was worried and scared. The last thing she wanted to do was bring up old hurts or add to his questions.

As she debated about just how much to share, something in his expression shifted. He looked resolute, almost as if he were preparing himself to hear worse news. "All right. I'm sorry, but Marie was worried about more than just putting her trust in you."

"More?" Jackson stuffed his hands in the front pockets of his jeans. "Is she concerned about her safety? I'm a cop. I would protect her no matter what."

"I think she knows that. But I don't think she was as concerned about her safety as much as her heart."

"LizBeth, Marie thinks I'm going to hurt her feelings?" He turned away and walked a few steps before pacing back to her. "I honestly don't know what I did wrong."

"Jackson, she was afraid you were going to leave Berlin."

"What did you tell her?"

"I told her I was afraid of you leaving, too. Especially since your leaving was inevitable."

He scowled. "That's what you told her when she came to you for help and reassurance?"

LizBeth flinched at his tone but she didn't back

down. What she had to share was important, and Jackson needed to put aside his feelings and concentrate on what she was telling him. "Marie asked for the truth, so the truth is what I gave her."

"I wish you wouldn't have been so blunt."

His mild criticism absolutely did not sit well with her. "I told Marie that I'd tell her the truth, and I didn't lie about that, Jackson. You are going to leave again."

"You make it sound like I'm going to leave without warning. Or without giving her a way to get in touch with me."

Since that was exactly what he'd done before, all LizBeth could do was stare at him.

"What happened back then has nothing to do with what's happening now," he said.

"You might think that, but I don't know if it's true. I still remember how confused and hurt I was. I waited for the mail each day, sure you were going to write. You never did."

"I was barely getting along. It wasn't until Roy found me and offered me a place to live that I stopped being afraid."

"I understand."

He either didn't hear her, or he was too deep in his own memories to care about hers. "Back then? Boy, I was so young. It took me about eight hours to realize that while I might be out of my house, I didn't have the first inkling of how to survive in the outside world. I can't believe you thought I'd somehow know where to get a piece of paper, an envelope and a stamp."

It took effort, but she reined in her temper. "Jackson, let's get back on track. You asked me about my conversation and I told you some of what was said."

He closed his eyes and hung his head. "You're right. I'm sorry. Please continue."

"Are you sure?"

"Of course. You're right. I'm making this about me, and that's wrong."

Her heart ached for him. Choosing her words with care, she said, "Like I said, I told Marie to trust you. I told her I was sure that you loved her very much and that if she wanted your help with your parents or even to leave, that you would understand and do whatever you could."

He nodded slowly. "I absolutely would. Did she say anything else?"

"Yes, she mentioned a man named Aaron and said that she didn't need your help, that he was former Amish and he was really kind and had helped other women leave."

"She's mentioned him to me, too. Is that when she left?"

"No, she left because I started asking her questions she couldn't answer. Questions about Aaron and the other girls' names. Jackson, Marie got really upset when I asked what happened to the other women and if she'd heard from any of them."

"What did she say?"

"It was obvious she hadn't thought beyond leaving her house. She got rattled and defensive when I kept asking her why she trusted this Aaron and how she was going to pay for food and rent."

"And then?"

"And then she left, Jackson. I offered to drive her home but I don't think she heard me—she was half-way out the door when I said it. I should have made her wait for me, but I was afraid she'd leave while I put on proper clothes."

"I did the same the other night. I was afraid to do anything to push her away." He ran a hand through his hair. "But I pushed her away anyway, didn't I?"

"What are you going to do now?"

"I'm going to call Mose and one of my friends at the station and see if she's come up with any information about this mysterious Aaron. And then, after double-checking that she hasn't already gone home, I'm going to ask for your help. I think we need to start looking for her."

She understood his fears, but LizBeth wondered if he was overreacting. "She might not have anything to do with your Jane Doe, Jackson. Marie might just be in a good old teenaged girl snit and hanging out at a friend's house. It might be as simple as that."

"I hope and pray that is the case," he said as he headed toward the door. "I'd love nothing better than to be accused of making a big deal out of nothing."

"Call me as soon as you can. I'll be ready."

He paused, and the look he gave her was so grateful, so intense, her heart skipped a beat. "*Danke,*" he murmured before walking out the door.

"You're welcome, Jackson." She knew right then that she'd probably do anything for him. She was starting to think that her heart still belonged to him—even after all this time.

"I really need to go to the bathroom, Aaron," Marie said. "You need to stop. I'm not kidding."

Looking annoyed, he swerved to the side of the road. "Fine. Let's go."

She looked around. "What are you talking about? There's nothing here."

He scanned the side of the road, then pointed to a cluster of overgrown bushes about five yards away. "Go there."

"There? Outside on the side of the road?"

He glared. "We have a long way to go, Marie. Do you really think I'm going to go to some rest stop for you?" His expression darkened. "Even if you were lying, you better go now, because I'm not going to stop again for another couple of hours."

"Fine." She darted toward the bushes, holding off the latest round of tears until her back was to him. There was no way she was going to cry in front of him again if she could help it.

With every foot of space between her and him, she felt as if she could breathe more easily. Sitting next to him in the car had been so horrible.

Thirty minutes after they'd left Berlin and he was driving on the highway, he'd told her to take off her *kapp*. She'd been such a fool. She'd stared at him in confusion. And had dared to ask him why she should do that.

He'd acted as if she'd asked the stupidest question on earth. "Because you wanted to be *Englisch,* right? It's time to remove that prayer cap."

Even though she'd been at gatherings where the girls had taken off their prayer coverings, being forced to do so felt scary. But then, everything about him had become scary.

Gone was the Aaron she'd thought she'd known. The man who joked around and teased and seemed to only want what was best for her. In his place was the man she knew now. He was cold, scary, and he acted as if she wasn't anything to him.

Quickly crouching behind the bush, she did her business, looking beyond in the faint hope that someone was nearby who could help her get away.

But, of course, all that was around was a bunch of prairie grass, a couple of random groups of bushes and a heavy feeling of isolation.

"Marie, get over here or I'm coming to you. If that happens, you're not going to like it."

She didn't doubt his words. After she'd started crying the second time, he offered to give her some medicine so she wouldn't be so scared. At first, she hadn't known what he meant, but when he opened the compartment in the car and pulled out a needle, Marie had shaken her head.

She'd been so afraid that he was going to jab her arm anyway, but he'd just laughed, saying she would change her mind soon. Everyone always did.

She'd known then that LizBeth had been very right. Marie had been foolish to never ask questions about what happened after he helped the other girls leave. Of course, he probably wouldn't have told her that this would happen, but at least he would've realized she was smart.

When she got close to him, he pointed to the car. Dutifully, she turned and walked to the passenger side and got in. Five minutes later, they were speeding south along the highway again and Aaron seemed almost pleasant.

"Your hair is prettier than I remembered. How long is it?"

"It falls to the center of my back."

"Take it down. I want to see it." When she hesitated, he lowered his voice. "Take your hair down, Marie. Do it now. I promise, you don't want to see what happens when you disobey."

With shaking hands, Marie did as he asked. And tried not to think about what else he was going to order her to do.

Chapter Nineteen

Jackson felt more clearheaded as he walked out of Liz-Beth's apartment. He'd gotten himself into such a state that he'd ignored his years of training and started reacting with only his emotions. He didn't blame himself—after all, he was worrying about his sister and scared to death he wasn't going to see her again.

Now, even though he was still shaken up, Jackson was able to look at the situation in a clearer, more levelheaded way. And what he realized was that he was too close to it. He needed to step back and give himself both some grace and support.

And he needed to do two things. The first was to check in with Mose Kramer and talk to him again about not only Marie's absence but also more about the cold case.

After nothing had come of his shot tire, other than Mose reckoned it had merely been a bored kid with a hunting rifle, Jackson had been reluctant to press him for more information. Nothing good was going to come from pushing around his weight and acting like he knew how to handle things because he was a big-city cop.

Now that he wanted Mose's help to find his sister, who had only been gone about twelve hours, Jackson knew he was going to have to use a little finesse. As easygoing as Mose was, he wasn't going to respond well to Jackson connecting A to B to Z and then demanding he drop everything to help.

And Jackson knew he wouldn't blame him if that was the case. He would respond the same way if some guy from another jurisdiction showed up and tried to tell him how to do his job.

That was why he pursued the second task first. He called Brian Klinger, his best friend at the Cincinnati Police Department. He and Brian had been in the same rookie class. And though they had gone down different paths—Jackson toward murders and homicides while Brian loved being a street cop and working in community relations—the two of them had always been good sounding boards for each other.

Pulling over into a parking lot, he gave Brian a call.

He answered on the second ring. "Klinger."

"Hey, it's me. You got a minute?"

"For you, I've got two. Hold a second." Put on hold, Jackson leaned back and looked at the scenery. He'd pulled into a bank parking lot. There were five cars in the lot, two bicycles parked off to the side and a horse and buggy hitched to a post near the back. The driver must have thought he would be right out, because he'd unhitched his horse, which was contentedly munching on some fresh grass just on the other side of the split rail fence.

Gazing at the horse, a dozen memories rose inside

him. To his surprise, they weren't all bad, either. He used to love caring for their two horses. When he was a boy, his father had carefully shown him how to curry-comb a horse's coat and gently clean its hooves. One time, their sweet mare Dolly had playfully head-butted his father, almost making him lose his balance. Jackson had held his breath, afraid his *daed* would hit the horse for her antics, but he'd just laughed and scratched Dolly in between her ears.

"Horses are truly the Lord's most beautiful creatures," he'd murmured. "We are blessed to have two of them. Blessed that they trust us, too. Jackson, you'd best take care of them and get to know their personalities. If you do that, they'll be your friends for life. Ain't so?"

Jackson had been so taken aback, he'd merely nodded. But it had certainly made an impression on him. He'd taken his father's words to heart and always made sure to give the horses time and attention each day.

When was the last time he'd spent any time with a horse, or even had the opportunity to rub its nose? Two years ago? Or was it four?

"Sorry about that," Brian said as he got back on the line. "I've been taking my lunch in this little diner and a couple of the kids I've been mentoring at the high school walked over to say hello."

That was Brian. He excelled in the kind of police work that Jackson had always been challenged by. "Everything good with them?"

"Good enough. One of the boys is working as a mechanic. I'm proud of him. For a while there, I'd been afraid he wasn't even going to graduate. Now he's living on his own and seems happy."

"That's a success story."

"I think so, too. At least it is for him, you know? I wish more kids I meet with would have such good news to share." He took a deep breath. "I'm good now. What's going on? How's your Jane Doe coming along?"

"That's why I'm calling. I think I need some help, both with her and with my sister." He took a deep breath and braced himself. "She went missing this afternoon."

"Missing? You sure?" His voice was all business.

"I'm not sure but it's a good possibility. She left a woman's apartment on her own and never made it home. I'm going to check into some possibilities but it's looking doubtful."

"Because she's Amish?"

"No, because she's Marie and my parents are my parents."

"Hey, buddy, I hate to break it to you, but even good girls take off to have some fun from time to time."

"I'm aware of that, but I also know the people involved. I'm not exaggerating when I say that showing up two or three hours late is not the kind of thing that would be tolerated by my parents. They give a whole new meaning to strict and unyielding."

"Okay, then. When do you need me to come up there?"

"As soon as you can get away. I still need to talk to the local sheriff but I can give Sergeant Gunther or the captain a call if you'd like. At least then you won't have to explain yourself."

"No need. I'm going to take time off."

Relief and gratitude filled Jackson, but he hesitated. "Brian, that's big of you, but this might not be a day or two thing."

"I know. Look, let me walk back to my car and get to the station. Text me your address and expect me tomorrow morning."

"Thanks. I owe you."

"Don't thank me for wanting to help track down a guy's sister. See ya."

He clicked off then, leaving Jackson shaking his head. Brian really was one in a million.

Feeling better already, he pulled out onto the road and headed toward the sheriff's office. For good measure, he started praying for the Lord's help, not only to find Marie, but to give him the strength he needed over the next few days. Things were about to get intense.

He could feel it in his bones.

"What's going on, LizBeth?" Ana, one of her part-time employees, asked.

"Hmm? Oh, nothing."

Ana pointed to the collection of cans that LizBeth had taken off the shelves to check expiration dates and reorganize. "You've been fussing with the same four cans for the last ten minutes. Either something's going on with you, or you need to tell me about this new way of organizing you've adopted."

Staring at the group of cans in front of her, LizBeth chuckled. "This is not a new way of anything. You're right, my mind is on something else today."

"Let me guess, he's tall, dark and handsome…and he just happens to be in town for a visit."

Even though her cheeks were heating with embarrassment, LizBeth chuckled. "You're right. Jackson is here and I have been seeing quite a bit of him."

Ana grinned. "I knew it. We ladies were all talking

about you two on Sunday after church. Fern thought
he was here to finally make up with his parents, but I
shook my head at that."

LizBeth wasn't exactly thrilled to be the focus of
that conversation, but she knew better than to chide
Ana for talking about her. Every group of women she'd
ever met liked to do that from time to time. Even forty-
year-old Old Order Amish women like Ana.

Besides, she was starting to realize that dwelling
on her problems alone wasn't exactly helping much.
"Jackson and I have been spending time together," she
admitted, "but I'm afraid it has less to do with our past
relationship than the police case he's working on."

Ana frowned slightly. "I'd forgotten that he's a police officer now. Fern didn't mention that."

LizBeth hated how Fern seemed to act as if she were
the authority about everything that happened around
Berlin. "Fern doesn't know everything, Ana."

"You might think that…but I could point out about
twenty people who feel differently." She waggled her
eyebrows up and down.

"You are funny," LizBeth said with a chuckle. "To
get back to Jackson, he's a cop down in Cincinnati and
specializes in solving cold cases."

"What are those?"

"Cases that don't get solved and eventually grow
cold and almost forgotten. He really enjoys it, I think."

"What's he doing up here?"

Since Jackson had never mentioned that his Amish
Jane Doe was a secret, she didn't feel too bad about
sharing the details of the case. Marie was missing and
he needed as much help as possible. "It's a little disturbing. I wouldn't want to upset you."

After double-checking that no one had entered the store that she wasn't aware of, Ana sat down on the recently swept wooden floor. "I'm tougher than you, LizBeth."

"Is that right?"

"How many chickens have you slaughtered for supper?"

LizBeth held up a hand. "None and point taken! Don't say another word."

"I'm just saying that I can take all kinds of gory details."

"Well, um, all right, then. Jackson came across a file from a murder that happened two years ago." When Ana leaned forward, obviously intrigued, LizBeth added, "I'm afraid there's a chance the woman might have something to do with this store."

Ana's eyes widened. "Do tell."

"The woman was found with one of our Daisy Bags."

Her eyes widened. "That means she was a customer."

"I thought the same thing at first, but Jackson said the victim might have simply gotten that bag from someone else or even found it somewhere."

Looking troubled, Ana nodded. "As much as I'd like to say that Busy only gave those bags to people who really deserved them, sometimes she just gave them to any customer." Frowning, she added, "That's what you get when you have a lot of *Englischer* tourists. You just don't know what will happen next."

"The woman wasn't an *Englischer*, Ana. She was Amish."

"*Nee*. Are they sure?"

"I think they're pretty sure. It seems this Amish

Jane Doe had a *kapp* and some other things Jackson said were Amish."

"I'm not proud of myself, because it shouldn't matter if she was Amish or *Englisch*...but somehow this news worries me more."

"I felt the same way. I wouldn't want any woman to be murdered but there's something about knowing that it might have been an Amish woman from our community that gives me chills."

Looking reflective, Ana murmured, "Well, I suppose it's some small comfort that it wasn't a woman from our area."

"Why would you say that? Don't forget, she had a Daisy Bag."

"That's true, but I canna think of any woman who's recently gone missing without jumping the fence for years now."

LizBeth paused. She'd been organizing more cans but she set them down, forgotten again. "Wait, you know of someone?"

Ana looked taken aback by her tone, but she nodded agreeably. "I think I do. Mary Borntrager. Did you ever meet her?"

Feeling the hair on the back of her neck prickle, LizBeth shook her head. "*Nee*. How old do you think she was when she went missing?"

"I don't know. Maybe seventeen or so?"

"Where did Mary live?"

"Hmm." Ana stilled for a moment before nodding. "She lived over in Charm, I think. I knew Mary because my next-door neighbor's cousin was Mary's *bruder* James, who worked at Kinsinger's Lumber."

It was a convoluted relationship but LizBeth had

no problem following along. Since so many Amish had both the same first and last names, one had to describe their relations so everyone could connect the dots. "What happened to Mary?"

"No one rightly knows for sure, I'm afraid." Ana crossed her arms over her chest. "One day James called off, saying that the family was out searching for her."

"And they never found her?"

"*Nee.*" Ana picked up a couple more cans, checked the dates stamped on the bottom and then placed them back on the shelf. "Of course, I was sure that she'd taken off. Some girls do that, you know."

LizBeth nodded. "Maybe she did run off, but her family didn't want to admit it or something."

"I don't think that's likely. James said she was a friendly sort. A product of her family. No one thought she ran away because she had no other choice."

"This happened two years ago?"

"*Jah*, two. Maybe three." She shrugged. "Thereabouts." Ana narrowed her eyes. "LizBeth, why do you look so concerned?"

"What did Mary look like?"

"I don't know. Like any other Amish girl, I guess."

LizBeth pressed. "I mean, was she big, small? Brown eyes or blue?"

"Well, now. From what I remember, she was a pretty thing. Slim and always smiling. I couldn't say what color of eyes she had, though."

"I guess not." LizBeth tried to hide her disappointment. After all, it wasn't Ana's fault that she didn't remember Mary's eye color.

"I rarely notice the color of someone's eyes unless they're real unusual, you know?"

"I am the same way. Don't worry about it."

"*Jah*, eyes don't always make an impact. Not like a person's hair. I recall that Mary's was the palest blond. Looked almost white, you know? She was a pretty thing."

Feeling sick, LizBeth stood up. "Ana, look over the store for a few, would you? I need to do something in my office."

"You take your time, dear. I'd say you need a moment to get your head back together." She smiled sweetly. "Besides, there's no one here."

"Thanks."

The moment she closed the office door behind her, LizBeth rested her head on the door and tried to make sense of everything she'd just heard. She knew she shouldn't jump to conclusions, but everything was sure pointing to Jackson's investigation.

But was she just so anxious to play detective she was imagining a connection where there wasn't one? Also, did she dare bother Jackson when he had something far more urgent to focus on? Even if the Amish Jane Doe was Mary, Jackson might not care.

But what if it was? What if Mary's family had been both mourning the loss of her and crying about her disappearance all this time? Didn't that matter, too?

Just as she was about to start pacing, she felt the Lord's presence with her. It felt as if He were whispering in her ear, encouraging her to do the right thing.

And there really was only one right thing to do.

Picking up the phone, she dialed Jackson's number. If he was too busy to answer, she would leave a message.

All she knew was that all of this was out of her hands.

"Hello?" he answered.

"Jackson, I'm sorry to bother you, but I need to tell you something."

"About Marie?"

"No, about your Jane Doe."

"What about her?" His voice held noticeable disappointment.

"I think I just found out her name."

"Seriously? What is it?"

"Mary Borntrager." After another moment's hesitation, she quickly recounted her conversation with Ana. "Like I said, I don't know if it will help or not, but I didn't want to keep this news to myself."

"I see."

He didn't sound near as excited as she'd hoped. "What's wrong?"

"Nothing. It's just, well, I looked into the woman your friend Merv told me about and discovered that Charity had never been missing at all. She married a Mennonite and lives in Ashland. I had forgotten how many stories can get spun up in our small community."

"Rumors do happen, but usually there's some thread of truth to them, too. What if that's the case here?"

"You're right. Forgive me. I appreciate the call. Stay at the store, okay? I'll be right there."

After they disconnected, she breathed a sigh of relief. She'd followed her heart and His wishes. It had been the right choice.

Now all she had to do was wonder if her call had helped or if she'd directed Jackson toward another dead end.

Chapter Twenty

Aaron had to fill up his car's gas tank. He'd pulled off the highway with a stream of curses. His words had certainly shocked Marie, but not near as much as the way his personality had changed. For the last hour, he'd been acting even more irrational and mean. He'd yelled at Marie for not saying a word, then when she did mutter something, he would scream at her for being disrespectful.

She'd cried and pleaded for hours. Eventually, she turned numb…and then had finally decided it was time she got stronger. Filled with thoughts about Jackson's investigation, Marie realized that no policeman was going to appear out of thin air and wave Aaron off the road. She was going to have to do whatever it took to save herself.

When he exited the highway, Marie knew the Lord had listened to her prayers. He was giving her a chance. Now all she had to do was believe in herself enough to take it.

She noticed immediately that the gas station was fairly busy. There were at least six other vehicles in the vicinity, and all but one of them were driven by men. She was grateful for that.

Surely, one of them would intervene if she cried out for help.

Of course, Marie knew her chances for escape were slim. But she had no desire to get to wherever Aaron was taking her. She felt all the way down to her bones that if Aaron got her to her destination, something terrible was going to happen.

Even more important to her heart, she couldn't bear the thought of being another victim that Jackson had to investigate. It would ruin him.

During the few hours of their journey, ever since she'd had to relieve herself on the side of the road, Marie had stopped attempting to reason with Aaron. It was as if she'd needed that humiliating experience— all while seeing that Aaron hadn't been affected in the slightest—to understand that she was completely at his mercy.

But now, as they came to a stop at the gas pump, she had a sixth sense that this was her last opportunity to escape.

Aaron turned off the ignition and opened the driver's side door. Knowing that she couldn't act even the slightest bit interested in the world outside his car, she sat listlessly and only looked straight ahead.

"Glad you're finally learning to mind me," he said in a low mean tone. "And just in case you're thinking of doing something stupid, let me warn you now—don't even try it. Bad things happened to the last girl who tried to run away."

She didn't reply, but her insides were seething. This was the type of man he was. A bad man. A terrible one. A man so awful that he was acting as if his last victims were nothing but other "girls" whom he'd escorted down south.

Aaron would likely never realize it, but his last warning had given her the strength she needed to try anything. She'd rather be hurt or even killed while trying to escape instead of hoping she survived whatever he had in store for her.

When his back was turned, she carefully unlatched the seat belt and said a prayer. It already seemed as if the Lord was with her—He'd put the gas tank on the driver's side of the car instead of hers.

Please, God, help me escape and please give one of these people around us the strength and fortitude to help me, she prayed silently.

Then, knowing there was nothing else to do, she threw open the door, screaming as loud as she possibly could.

As she'd hoped, every person in the entire gas station stopped whatever they were doing and turned to her.

"Help me! This man has taken me against my will!"

Using every bit of courage she had, she got to her feet and hurried toward the nearest vehicle. "Help me, please."

"Marie!" Aaron called out. "What are you doing?"

She ran to the next vehicle, screaming loud enough to prevent anyone from ignoring her. "Please! Someone, anyone, help!"

That last plea seemed to shake everyone from their shock. "Miss?" a big, burly trucker said. "You're serious, aren't you?"

Just as she showed the trucker her black eye she'd

received when she hadn't taken her hair down fast enough, Aaron grabbed her shoulder. "Be quiet, Marie," he said under his breath.

"*Nee!* No way am I going anywhere with you. Don't touch me!"

Another pair of men approached. "I think you'd best leave her alone," one of them said to Aaron. "I don't know what's going on, but she's obviously not eager to go anywhere with you."

Aaron smiled, but his attempt made him look pretty slimy instead of more trustworthy. "You have this all wrong. She's my girlfriend and we had a fight. But it's—"

"That's not true! I was walking home and he tricked me into getting into the car with him. I've been trying to escape for hours." She started crying even though she had wanted to be so strong. "Please believe me."

The burly trucker grabbed Aaron and positioned his arms behind his back. "I do believe you, honey. Don't you worry about that." When Aaron struggled and attempted to talk, the trucker seemed to tighten his grip. "I'd shut up if I were you."

It was almost over. Wrapping her arms around herself, Marie stared at the group of men standing around them. "Please, would someone call the police?"

"Already on it, honey," a woman who'd been standing in the background said. "I dialed 911 the moment I heard what you said."

"Thank you. Thank you all so much." Tears filled her eyes as she realized just how close she'd come to being Aaron's hostage indefinitely. "I've been so scared."

One of the muscular guys gestured to the metal

bench next to the entrance to the gas station's large convenience store. "Why don't you go have a seat, Miss? My boy here will go get you a Coke. You look a little worse for wear."

Aaron struggled against the man's restraints. "All of you are overreacting. She and I just had a little argument. It's nothing more than that."

"I reckon the police can decide that for themselves," one of the men said. "But I'm of the mind that no woman fights like that unless she's got something to fight for."

The kind woman approached as they heard the distant hum of the police sirens. "Come sit down, Miss. The police will be here soon."

"*Danke.*" Marie hardly recognized her voice it was so strained. "I mean, thank you."

"No need to thank us, dear. It's a blessing that we were all here to help."

"A blessing, indeed," she agreed, though she felt it was more like a miracle. Only the Lord could have provided both her opportunity and the amazing people who helped her escape.

"Lapp," Jackson said into the phone as he straightened. He'd been in Marie's bedroom, searching for anything to help him learn where she might have gone.

"We've got him," Brian said.

"Got who?"

"Aaron Zook. And more importantly, Marie is okay."

Stunned, he sat down on the side of Marie's bed. "You found Marie?"

Brian chuckled softly over the line. "I'd say it was

more like she found us. You're going to be so proud of that little sister of yours, Jackson. When Aaron pulled into a truck stop, she ran out of his sedan and screamed for help. About a half-dozen truckers came to her rescue. It's on tape, too! I can't wait to see it."

Marie was okay. She'd gotten free. The cops had the man who'd abducted her. Jackson closed his eyes in relief. He'd been so afraid. And while the news that his worst fear had actually happened sank in, he dwelled instead on his friend's words. Marie had been found and she was okay.

"I think you're going to need to backtrack," he said after taking a deep breath. "Where is she? And is she hurt? Is she in the hospital? Which one?"

"Hold on, buddy. One step at a time. She's in a little hamlet just south of Columbus at the police station."

"Where?"

"Pleasant Corners. Got it?" he asked.

Jackson wasn't sure if he did or didn't. To his shame, he was realizing that he really had been preparing himself for the worst. "You're sure she's okay?"

"I promise, Jack. I wouldn't sugarcoat it if she was hurt." His voice warmed. "I was told to tell you that your little sister's all settled in a lieutenant's office. Last I heard, someone got her some hot tea and a package of cookies or something. She's okay."

"She's not hurt," he reminded himself again.

"No. She's shaken up and asking for you, though. When can you get here?"

"Ninety minutes. I'll leave now." Right before he hung up, something occurred to him. "Hey, how come you're calling me?"

"Nine-one-one operator sent out the sheriff, who

sent word to the station because she's your sister. I was elected to give you a call."

"I'm glad, but why?"

"Because I'm halfway there, Jack. No way am I going to let you handle any of this on your own."

Suddenly, his whole body felt ten times lighter. "Thanks, see you soon."

Walking out of Marie's room, he was startled to see both of his parents standing in the hallway, looking anxious.

"We heard you on your cell phone," *Daed* said. "Do you have news?"

"I do. Marie has been found. She's okay."

"Praise God," *Mamm* said while his father closed his eyes in relief.

"I'm going to head down to see her," he said. "She should be back home by nightfall."

His father stared at him intently. "What happened? Did she run away?"

"No. I'm not sure about the particulars, but I'm fairly sure she was taken against her will."

Daed blinked. "Truly? She's only eighteen. How in the world did she get free?"

"I don't know the whole story. What I am hearing is that Marie was very brave."

Releasing a ragged sigh, his father placed a heavy hand on his shoulder. "Jackson, I have to tell ya this before you go."

"Yes, *Daed*?"

"Years ago, I was too hard on you. I knew it, but I was too weak to be a better man. It was my fault that you ran away and I've carried that burden with me, knowing it was no one else's to share."

Everything his father was saying was true. But now that he'd been back in Berlin and reunited with Marie, his parents and LizBeth, Jackson realized he didn't harbor all that pain and resentment anymore. Instead, he'd found forgiveness. Not just for himself, but for his parents' actions, too.

"We don't need to talk about this, *Daed.* It's all in the past."

"Hold on. What I'm trying to say is I realize now that the Lord has given us grace again." He swallowed hard. "*Nee*, given *me* grace. He's brought you back to us, and even brought you to Marie when she needed you the most. I'm grateful for you."

Overcome by hearing the words he'd never imagined his father would say, Jackson hugged his father hard. "*Danke.*"

After releasing his father, he hugged his *mamm*, then pulled out his keys. "I've got to go. I'll do my best to make sure Marie gets home tonight. I promise."

Eyes shining, his mother nodded.

She believed him. No, she believed *in him*.

That meant the world.

Chapter Twenty-One

Two hours after Jackson had called and asked her to meet him in Pleasant Corners, LizBeth exited the highway and followed the directions on her phone to the local police station.

When he'd called from his vehicle, filling her in on Marie's rescue and Aaron being taken into custody, she'd been near tears. Like Jackson, she'd feared the worst for Marie. She was so grateful the girl had been found.

Of course, she didn't know the whole story—maybe Marie had been hurt, emotionally or physically. If that was the case, LizBeth was determined to help Marie recover as much as the girl allowed. Maybe, in time, Marie would even learn to trust her and consider Liz-Beth a friend.

The police station was a one-story nondescript brick building. When she walked in, an officer in uniform looked up from his computer. "May I help you?"

"Yes. My name is LizBeth Troyer. My friend Jackson Lapp asked me to come to escort his sister home."

Smiling slightly, the man stood up. "They're in the captain's office. Follow me."

She hadn't taken the time to do much more than brush her hair before heading to her car and driving south. Hearing her tennis shoes squeak on the linoleum made her aware of just how casually she was dressed. Maybe she should have changed into jeans and an oxford cloth shirt? Her gym shorts, T-shirt and old sneakers felt out of place.

However, when she walked into the room and caught sight of Jackson and Marie sitting together, all thoughts about appropriate dress dissipated in an instant.

Jackson was holding both of his younger sister's hands and talking to her quietly. Marie was wearing the same dark pink dress she'd worn when she'd visited LizBeth that morning. However, her *kapp* was nowhere in sight and her blond hair fell down her back, almost reaching her waist. Seeing Marie's beautiful hair uncovered and in such disarray spurred LizBeth's eyes to tear up again. LizBeth still remembered how awkward and almost exposed she'd felt the first time she went out in public without a prayer covering. That decision had been hers, though. Marie, on the other hand, had likely been forced to take her hair down by her abductor. LizBeth couldn't imagine how traumatizing that must have been.

Sitting beside Marie, Jackson appeared calm, but she could tell his expression was strained. He was wearing tan cotton khakis, dark loafers and a blue button-down shirt. He looked crisp and neat. She realized he was likely wearing his work uniform. For the first time, she was seeing him through a new lens—

maybe even the way the rest of the world saw him. As a cop instead of just Jackson.

When Jackson glanced her way, he stood up and crossed the room. "Thanks for coming, LizBeth," he said as he reached for her hand.

She smiled at him, trying to convey how much she felt for him in her eyes. "Of course. I'm glad you called."

He looked as if he wanted to say more but simply nodded.

Knowing Jackson needed a moment, LizBeth turned to his sister. "How are you, Marie?"

She shrugged. "I'm okay, I think."

"I'm glad."

When neither said another word, LizBeth looked up at Jackson. "Are you hanging in there?" she whispered.

"I'm trying to." He ran a hand through his hair. "Uh, right before you arrived, Marie and I were talking. I think the reality of what could have happened is sinking in for both of us." He paused, visibly trying to collect himself. "It's hard not to keep thinking about what could've happened if Marie hadn't been so fierce and brave."

LizBeth felt another surge of affection for Jackson. Even now, when it was obvious that he would love nothing more than to scream or hit something, he was doing his best to lift up his sister and concentrate on her needs. LizBeth was so proud of him.

"I can't wait to hear about your fierceness, Marie," she said lightly.

"I'll be glad to tell you about it on our way back home."

"When would you like us to be on our way, Jackson?"

"As soon as possible. Marie is anxious to get home and I… Well, I have some work to do."

She guessed he was anxious to talk to this Aaron—about both Marie and his cold case. She smiled. "Then I'm ready whenever you are, Marie."

Pure relief filled the girl's expression as she stood up. "I'm ready now." Heading to the door, she added, "I'm gonna run to the bathroom again, Jackson."

"Of course. We'll be right here." After his sister left, Jackson reached for her hand again. "LizBeth, I can't thank you enough for coming down here. With Aaron in lock up here, I can't take the time to escort Marie myself."

She squeezed her fingers around his larger palm. "I wouldn't want to be anywhere else." That was the truth, too. She wanted to be here for both Marie and Jackson.

"In that case, what can I do for you? Would you like some more time to rest before getting back in the car?" He looked around the room. "I bet I could find you something to drink. I'm sure there are some water bottles around here somewhere."

"I'll run to the ladies' room, but then I'll be good." She lowered her voice. "If it's okay with you, I thought we'd take the back roads home. If Marie wants to stop or get something to eat, we'll be able to do that more easily."

"I think that's perfect."

"I better get ready, then," she said as she stood up.

"Hold on a sec." He got to his feet and then, to her surprise, wrapped his arms lightly around her and kissed her on the lips.

When he stepped back, she smiled. "What was that for?"

"I don't want to go another day without letting you know that I care about you."

Her heart felt like it was suddenly beating a whole lot faster. "Jackson?"

"I know, I know. It's the wrong time to make a declaration or for either of us to even make promises. I just wanted to make sure you knew how I felt."

"In that case, maybe you should kiss me again," she joked.

But just as it looked like he was about to lean down and do exactly that, the door opened. "Guess what? They have sodas down the hall," Marie said.

Pulling away from him, LizBeth grinned. "A soda sounds perfect. I'll go get one of those myself," she said in a rush before hurrying out of the room.

Marie had seemed relieved to not be heading back on the interstate. However, it was obvious that she was still rattled and reeling from her experience.

LizBeth knew she'd probably already shared her story with both the local law enforcement personnel and her brother, so she elected not to pry. Instead, she turned on some music and drove the back roads. Every so often she would comment about a pretty flower bed or an unusual-looking building or restaurant.

Marie seemed to appreciate that. Sometimes she'd comment on whatever LizBeth pointed out. Other times, she simply nodded.

But then, when they were about halfway through the drive, Marie pointed to a favorite ice-cream spot that had a bright vintage-looking orange-and-white-swirled ice-cream sign. "Can we stop, do you think?"

"I think that sounds like a fantastic idea. I love ice cream."

"Me, too."

She pulled into a parking place on the side, and they exited. Marie seemed just as eager as she was to stretch her legs. Thankfully, there wasn't a long wait, and minutes later they were both holding orange-and-vanilla-swirled cones.

The day was perfect for eating ice cream. Warm enough that the treat helped cool them off, but not so hot that the ice cream melted down the sides of the cone.

"Your brother used to take me to an ice-cream shop in downtown Berlin," she said.

"Which one?"

"It's long gone, I'm afraid." Remembering some of the flavors they offered, LizBeth added, "I don't think it was a great fit for a town where most people prefer chocolate, vanilla or strawberry."

Marie grinned. "Not me. I like all kinds."

"I do, too." She took another bite of the frosty concoction. "What's your favorite? I'm afraid mine is still vanilla, unless it's a swirl cone like this."

"I like anything with peanut butter or chocolate."

"You could've gotten chocolate here."

"Maybe next time. This is good."

Noticing that Marie was almost finished, LizBeth said, "If you're hungry, you can get another cone. Or we can stop someplace else and get a real meal."

"I'm all right. This is fine."

"If you change your mind later, you can let me know."

"I will." She took a swipe of the dessert with her tongue, then said, "When Aaron was driving me on the highway, all I could think about were all the things I haven't yet done."

Oh, but that broke her heart. "I would've done the same thing."

"Would you?" Marie stared at her intently. "What else would you have thought about?"

The question felt out of the blue—but maybe not.

"I'm not really sure," she admitted. "I would like to think I would've prayed and counted my blessings, but maybe I would've also thought about the things I regretted." She pursed her lips. "Or I might have been so scared and upset, I wouldn't have thought about much at all."

"At first I was really scared. Aaron was so mean—and he was acting so different from how he used to. I didn't understand what was happening. But once I did, all I could think about was how to get away."

"It was the right choice. You did get away, Marie. You and the Lord worked together."

"Sometimes I was even afraid for him to stop," she added, sounding even more strained. "Because if he did, then I'd have to do whatever he wanted me to do."

Her heart felt like it was about to leap out of her chest. She was fighting tears, fighting the need to pull Marie into her arms. Even fighting the urge to ask her to stop, because thinking about this sweet girl worrying about such things was hard to do.

"I don't think there was a wrong thing to do, Marie."

"I'm not so sure about that, LizBeth."

"I am."

She looked down at her feet. "I almost don't want to go home because I don't want to talk about it."

"Then don't. Tell everyone that you need time. They'll understand."

"But what if they don't? What if they won't leave me alone until I tell them the whole story?" Marie's voice turned more stressed. "What if I give in and tell *Mamm* and *Daed* all about what happened? What do you think my parents will say, then? Or the bishop?"

"I think they'll be mighty glad you are home safe."

"*Nee*, you don't understand, LizBeth." Marie looked her in the eye. "What if everyone says I said and did the wrong things? What if they decide I'm a horrible person and all of this was my fault?"

LizBeth was taken aback. She'd never imagined that would be a concern...but then she remembered that Marie was just a young sheltered Amish teenage girl. She was used to always being judged and ordered about.

And maybe, at times, found wanting. After all, Jackson had felt the same way.

She took a deep breath, looking to find the right words. Needing to be honest and still helpful. She wasn't sure if she was ever going to have those words. All she could do was speak from her heart and hope for the best.

"First of all, I don't think anyone is going to say that. I can promise you that no one cared about anything but you and your safety. Not even your parents. Not even the bishop." Looking her directly in the eye, she added, "But even if someone did have something to say, I would try not to let it bother me."

"Really?"

"Really. Because no one was in that car with you," she continued in a firm tone. "No one but you *really* knows what that car ride was like, and Lord willing, they won't ever know."

Still not looking entirely convinced, Marie shrugged.

"Marie, honey, look at me." When her pretty blue eyes—so like Jackson's—stared back at her, LizBeth added the most important piece to the pep talk. "The reason no one else's opinion matters is because there's already one person who was there with you and already knows what you said."

"Aaron."

"He was there, but he wasn't who I was thinking of. It was God, Marie. He was there. He helped you be strong. He gave you the tools to survive and be brave and escape. It doesn't matter what I, or Jackson, or your parents, or anyone in the whole world thinks about what you did or should've done. That's because He's already given you His blessing."

A tear formed in her eye. "You sound so sure."

"Honey, look what happened. You survived and we're sitting here eating ice cream. If that isn't our dear Lord showing His love for you, I don't know what is."

At last, some of the darkness in Marie's face faded. "I am sitting here, aren't I?"

"Absolutely. I know the memories of what happened aren't going to be easy to handle. But if you try to re-member this moment, maybe it will be a little easier one day."

And just like that, Marie threw herself into LizBeth's arms and hugged her tight. LizBeth rubbed her back and swallowed the surge of emotion she was feeling.

And then she closed her eyes and returned her hug, thanking God all the while for keeping Marie safe. And, at last, for bringing Jackson back into her life as well.

Chapter Twenty-Two

After seeing Marie and LizBeth off, Jackson got himself a glass of water and spoke once again to Phillip, his sergeant back in Cincinnati. He also knew Brian was on his way, and that he would be the one transporting Aaron back to CPD, if that was needed.

Because local law enforcement had apprehended Aaron and taken Marie under their wing, Jackson offered to let the captain who'd arrived on the scene take the lead. Of course, that was really a formality.

Captain Branch was a burly guy about fifty years old. His hair was already snow-white and he had piercing light blue eyes. He was also former military and looked like he still did physical training on a daily basis. He was as far from an older cop enjoying a steady diet of fast-food as a man could get.

"Hey, Jackson, how you doing?" Captain Branch asked as he entered the room.

They shook hands. "Better, now that I've seen my sister."

"I would say I can't imagine what's been going

through your head, but I'm afraid I can." He grimaced. "I wouldn't wish that on my worst enemy."

Since the pain he'd been feeling was still fresh, Jackson didn't quite agree. "I would usually say the same, except I fear that wishing a bit of suffering on an enemy sounds pretty good right now." He smiled, just so the captain wouldn't think he was a total jerk.

Branch chuckled. "I hear what you're saying, buddy. Now, about this Aaron Zook. I'm planning to take the lead—but did I hear right that another cop from CPD should be joining us momentarily?"

Jackson nodded. "His name is Brian Klinger, and he's both a fellow officer and a friend of mine. He texted about an hour ago. He was ninety minutes out. Hopefully he'll be here soon."

"And why is he here again?"

"I've been working on a cold case the last couple of weeks." Briefly, he summarized what he'd found and the steps he'd taken so far.

Branch whistled low. "I'm assuming you think Aaron Zook is your guy?"

Jackson weighed his words carefully. "I won't know for certain until we interview him, but it's a definite possibility. But since my sister is involved and I'm now emotionally connected, I don't want anything to jeopardize that case. The last thing I want is for a judge or jury to say my involvement is a conflict of interest."

"Roger that. All right. I'll take the lead. You stay silent. When Brian arrives, he can help us circle back to the Amish Jane Doe case and then you can take over." He paused. "Do you have a problem with any of that?"

"No." They were about to take part in a complicated dance, but it was doable. He was glad both Brian and

Captain Branch were taking care to dot every *i* and cross every *t*. Those steps would cover a lot of people's backsides if the investigation ever fell under scrutiny.

He held out his hand again. "I appreciate the way you're handling everything. You didn't have to be so flexible."

"We're all in the same boat, right? Besides, this guy is too slick for his own good. I can't wait to make him squirm a little bit."

"You and me both."

Ten minutes later, Jackson followed Branch into the interrogation room. He'd purposely refrained from looking in the one-way window beforehand— he'd wanted his first glimpse of the guy to be in person. He'd wanted to be able to look him in the eye and see his response.

Now, however, he was wondering if that had been the right call. Aaron Zook was older than he'd imagined and his expression was both smug and calculating. Jackson's first reaction was being chilled. Aaron Zook was a dangerous man, and his little sister had come very close to being harmed.

As they'd agreed upon, Captain Branch took the lead. "Hello, Mr. Zook. My name is Captain Branch. This is Officer Lapp." Branch took the chair directly across from Aaron. Jackson stayed standing, remaining by the door.

Aaron barely spared Jackson a second look, which suited him just fine. Instead, he glared at the captain. "I've been waiting in here almost two hours."

"I know," Branch said.

As if he was feeling even more empowered, Aaron folded his arms across his chest and spoke more belligerently. "I don't know what you think was going on, but I'm here to tell you that none of what that girl was saying is true."

"Oh? And what was she saying?"

"You know, that she was with me against her will. You could talk to anyone back in her hometown. They'd tell you we are friends. She just wanted some attention."

"What do you mean by attention?"

And so it continued. Aaron essentially made Marie sound like a flirtatious liar all while digging himself in deeper. Jackson was glad for his experience as an MP in the army. He'd learned to conceal his emotions—especially when someone he knew was involved. Otherwise, he would have either bit his lip until it was bleeding or worn such an expression of distaste that Aaron would have realized he was emotionally involved.

Just as Captain Branch began reciting the litany of charges being filed against Aaron, Brian strode through the door.

He barely did more than nod in Jackson's direction before taking the empty seat. Brian looked every bit the successful detective he was. He was wearing a suit and polished shoes, and his good looks played off his cool expression.

"Mr. Zook, I'm Detective Brian Klinger from the Cincinnati Police Department."

Almost immediately, most of Aaron's bluster faded away. "Why are you here?"

"We have reason to believe that your transporting of Marie Lapp was not the first instance of you kidnapping and abetting in human trafficking."

"Yeah, right."

Brian stared at him until Aaron's smug smile faded. "I don't joke about sex traffickers, Mr. Zook. I also don't drive two hours north to talk to felons unless I have a good reason."

And just like that, everything in the interrogation shifted. Aaron started looking afraid, Captain Branch appeared to almost relax and Jackson faded further into the background. Then Brian went in for blood.

He began firing questions like lightning, barely allowing Aaron time to reply before switching avenues and asking about the man's past.

One hour went by. Aaron began to sweat and asked for a glass of water.

Jackson got him a paper cup and then returned to his position by the door.

And still the questions continued, when suddenly Aaron snapped. "All I had to do was get to know the women I was asked to meet and transport them to Cincinnati. That's it. I didn't kill anyone. And it sure wasn't my plan."

"Whose was it?" Branch asked.

"Fern."

"Fern who?" Brian asked. "And don't try to tell me you don't know."

Aaron didn't even hesitate for a full minute. "Fern Hershberger."

Jackson froze. That name was familiar. Was it just because Hershberger was a common Amish name? Or was it Fern that stuck in his mind?

Brian raised one eyebrow. "Her name is Fern, you say?"

"Yeah. Weird, right? She has connections with a

trafficker in Cincy. The guy paid her good money if she gave him a pretty, clean Amish girl once or twice a year."

"How did she choose the girls?"

"I don't know. I didn't care."

Brain glanced up at Jackson. Jackson mouthed, *Where*.

"Where is she?"

Aaron rolled his eyes. "Where do you think? Amish country."

"You need to be more specific."

"Fine. In Berlin. She works at a Podunk market part-time."

And that was it. He'd heard LizBeth mention Fern as one of her employees. Things had just gotten more complicated.

Instead of heading down to Cincinnati, he was headed back to Berlin once again.

Chapter Twenty-Three

Marie had never felt more alone than the moment LizBeth pulled onto her house's long winding gravel driveway. Within a few moments, LizBeth would no doubt say goodbye and drive back to her own life.

And Marie would be back where she'd been before Aaron Zook had come into her life—stuck at home. Once again, her only option to leave was to get married.

Which meant her husband could then be the one to tell her what to do.

Though Jackson had carefully explained why he couldn't accompany her home, his absence still hurt. There was a part of her that wondered if her brother would ever put her first. It was sure starting to feel like that would never happen.

Her pulse raced and it felt hard to breathe. "LizBeth, can we stop for a moment?"

"Of course." Looking alarmed, LizBeth tapped on the brakes and stopped the car near a pair of oak trees. "You okay?"

She tried to catch her breath. "I don't know."

LizBeth unbuckled Marie's seat belt, then pressed her palm on the middle of Marie's back to motion her forward. "Easy now. I don't want you fainting on me."

"I'm not going to faint."

"Just take a moment, Marie. Breathe deep." After Marie inhaled and exhaled, LizBeth patted her back again. "That's right. One more time."

Seconds passed. Eventually, she felt her heartbeat slow. When she leaned back in her seat, Marie realized she felt clearheaded again. Well, as clearheaded as she was able to feel at the moment. "I'm better now."

Still looking concerned, LizBeth unbuckled her seat belt as well. "It's okay if you're not. You don't have to be."

"I'm scared to see my parents," she blurted.

LizBeth's eyes filled with tenderness. "I can understand that. Are you afraid they'll get mad at you?"

"I know they will be. There's no doubt in my mind about that."

Thankfully, LizBeth didn't try to say she was making things up. Instead, she waited a few seconds, then asked, "Do you want me to come inside with you?"

"*Nee.* That might only make things worse." Liz-Beth would serve as a reminder of how much Marie could change one day. Her parents might even view her as a threat.

Thankfully, LizBeth didn't act offended or hurt by Marie's statement. "All right. Well, how about this? Do you want to practice what you're going to say?"

"Practice, like right now?"

"Absolutely." She smiled. "I know it sounds strange,

but sometimes if I practice saying the words, it doesn't sound quite as scary when I say them out loud for real."

"I couldn't. I mean, I can't." When LizBeth just stared at her, Marie sputtered, "I… I don't know what I'm going to say to them. I might just cry."

Still studying her intently, LizBeth said, "This might not help, but your brother told me once that nothing really good is ever easy. It might help if you are able to speak your mind and be honest with your parents."

That was a nice thought, but Marie figured all speaking her mind would do was guarantee a worse punishment.

But she didn't see a reason to share that with Liz-Beth. It wasn't her fault Marie's parents were so difficult. Spying the front door opening, she sighed. "You'd best drive forward. They see that I'm here."

"I don't care if they stand there for an hour. What matters is you, Marie. Are you sure you're ready to face them?"

LizBeth was being sincere. It was obvious that she'd turn off her car and wait for as long as Marie wanted. She knew right at that moment that God had brought LizBeth to her just to help her get through this day. "I think I have to be."

"Let's pray while I'm driving. I'll start. Dear, God."

"Dear, God."

"Please be with the Lapp family during this difficult time. Please put Your loving arms around Marie and hold her close. Help her recover from her ordeal. Please be with Jackson as he works to make sure Aaron never hurts another woman, and please be with Mr. and Mrs. Lapp. Help them focus on the love for their children and the blessings they've been given. Help them find the strength to listen instead of talk, to understand instead of incriminate. Help this family heal. In Your name, Amen."

"Amen," Marie repeated.

Stopping her car in front of the house, LizBeth said, "Marie, whatever you need, I'm here for you. Not just today, but tomorrow as well." More intently, she added, "Every day, if you'd like. Don't be afraid to ask."

"You're serious."

"I'm very serious. We're friends now, Marie. You are not alone."

She smiled at her. "*Danke*." Then she took a deep breath, opened the door and got out of the car. Marie's prayer had helped. Her words reminded her that she wasn't alone. Not by a long shot.

Finally meeting her mother's gaze, she said, "Hi. LizBeth brought me home."

"Oh, Marie!" her mother exclaimed as she pulled her into a beautiful hug. "Oh, my Marie." She clutched her so tightly that Marie had to try to catch her breath.

And then, to her shock, her father pulled her close and hugged her as well. She felt teardrops on her face and realized she was crying—and so was her father.

Tentatively, she wrapped her arms around her father and rested her forehead on his body. "I'm okay," she whispered. "I really am."

Two minutes later, her father released her with a shuddering breath and stood before her, wiping his eyes.

Marie realized she hadn't lied. She was okay. She was bruised, upset and confused about both what had happened and what her future involved. She'd made mistakes, yes, but she wasn't the only person who had.

And she was stronger than she'd ever thought she could be. So she wasn't perfect, not even close to being that.

However, the Lord didn't need her to be. He simply needed her to be who she was. That was enough.

Chapter Twenty-Four

Twenty-four hours after returning to Berlin, LizBeth felt as if everything that had happened with Marie had never taken place. Jackson was back in Cincinnati, and she knew he was occupied with both Aaron Zook and his Amish Jane Doe case.

Of course, all anyone outside their small group thought was that Marie had simply gone missing but was back at home, safe and sound. No doubt everyone had just thought she'd gotten a little wild in her *rumspringa*—which was a bit newsworthy, but not entirely out of the norm for Amish community gossip.

All of that meant her first few hours at Busy's felt more than a little surreal. It was only Friday. Tourists were pouring into town, and locals were intent on getting their errands done in order to avoid them.

Standing behind the counter, LizBeth tried her best to adjust. Everything seemed to be the same as it always had been at the shop. Customers wandered in to chat, others came with a long list and a short amount of time to complete their shopping, and the noisy, friendly tourists walked in in pairs and trios, each with wide eyes and money in their wallets.

By noon, they'd already made more money than they typically did after being open for eight hours. That knowledge more than made up for the fact that she was likely going to have to work a full hour after they closed to put everything to rights.

Thankfully, Fern was working. The lady had a talent for seeming folksy and approachable while being extremely efficient. Gifts like hers came in handy on busy days because she could charm the customers who wanted to chat without sacrificing sales or making people wait.

When Fern approached with Sally, one of their long-time best customers, LizBeth reached for the candles she was holding. "Fern, you should have asked for help."

"I might be older, but I can still carry stock around the store, LizBeth."

"Of course." With a wink at Sally, she added, "I didn't mean to offend."

Sally chuckled. "You'd best be careful, LizBeth. If you hurt Fern's feelings, you might lose her—and a great many of your customers, too."

"Surely not," she joked. "You'd not come in to see me?"

"I would, but maybe not as much." Smiling at the fifty-year-old woman, Sally winked. "Fern knows all the gossip, you see."

"I do see."

Fern looked mildly affronted. "I don't gossip. I only share stories."

"Stories about things women shouldn't be doing!" Sally chirped.

"I've been missing out, Fern," LizBeth teased. "All we ever talk about is the weather and what jobs to do around the store."

Still looking serious, Fern crossed her arms over her chest. "That is because you're an upstanding woman, LizBeth. You always have been."

"I've tried, but I've strayed a time or two," she joked. When Fern's expression didn't lighten, LizBeth realized that it might have been a good thing she and Fern had always kept their conversations centered around work. Stepping to the register, she asked, "Sally, are you ready to check out now?"

"I am, dear." Looking adorably alarmed, she quipped, "I need to leave before I buy out the store!"

LizBeth smiled at her joke and began to ring everything up. "Fern, would you mind going to the back and getting a box for the candles?"

Without a word, Fern did as she was asked and soon disappeared into the storage room.

Only when Fern was completely out of sight did Sally exhale. "I'm sorry to get Fern on her high horse, LizBeth. I hope she won't make the rest of your day a difficult one. That would be horrible."

Sally was acting as if Fern's opinion was something to be conscious of. "I don't think she's upset. Do you?"

"Probably not." She lowered her voice. "It's just that even when she and I were younger, Fern had a way of making one regret indiscretions."

This was news to LizBeth. "Really? I had no idea," she murmured as she wrapped each of Sally's candles in old newspaper.

After glancing to make sure the door was closed, Sally leaned close. "Once, a rumor was even going around that Fern was responsible for a woman jumping the fence."

"How could that be?"

"She has ways, LizBeth."

"Such as?" She didn't want to gossip, but Sally was truly making it sound as if Fern were an awful person.

Sally shook her head. "I can't talk about that. She'll be back any second."

And sure enough, Fern appeared not ten seconds later, her arms filled with two boxes. "I weren't sure which would be better, so I brought up two, LizBeth."

"I think that's a *gut* idea. Why don't you see which box works better." Turning to Sally, LizBeth added, "It will be eighty-four dollars today."

Sally handed her four twenties and a five. "Here you go, dear." After warily glancing at Fern, Sally added, "Do you still have a jar for widows and orphans, dear?"

"Of course." Fern pointed to a Mason jar with a slot cut out of the metal lid. "It's right here, like it always is."

Sally's smile was strained. "Oh, yes. Yes, of course. Put the change in there, please."

"*Danke*, Sally," Fern murmured.

Looking slightly relieved, Sally smiled again. "Of course, dear. Always happy to help."

Five minutes later, LizBeth was holding the door open for Sally as she hurried out, the big box filling her arms.

After the woman left, she looked over at Fern, who was back at work, organizing shelves. "Sally was in a strange mood today, don't-cha think? Or was it just me?"

"It weren't just you. She can be flighty at times. I'm guessing this was one of those days."

Deciding not to overthink it, LizBeth nodded. "I guess you're right. Well, it's four o'clock, so it's time for you to be on your way."

"*Danke*, LizBeth. You're a *gut* boss."

"I appreciate that, Fern, but we both know I'll never be as good as my grandmother was."

Fern smiled. "Oh, I think you might be. Busy weren't always perfect you know."

"None of us are, right? I was always glad about that, too. It means I'm in good company."

"To be sure." She patted LizBeth on the arm as she retrieved her purse from under the counter. "You're a good'un, LizBeth Troyer."

"Even though I'm not Amish?"

Fern's friendly smile faded. "Not everyone who is Amish is good. Believe me, I know," she said before turning and walking briskly out the door.

The bells jangled on the door again as it snapped shut, and the ringing almost sounded as if they were raising an alarm. Staring through the large plate glass windows at the number of people walking by, LizBeth tried to find Fern but she'd already gone.

For the first time, she was almost glad about that. Maybe it was the way Sally seemed so skittish around her, but it had surely raised some questions as far as LizBeth was concerned.

She'd never imagined Fern was the type of person who might judge others harshly. She didn't know if that was because Fern was older, because she was Amish or because she'd always been pleasant and helpful to LizBeth.

But then again, she hadn't really conversed with Fern about anything beyond the shop. Shaking her head, LizBeth reminded herself there was nothing wrong with being simply coworkers. One didn't need to be best friends with someone in order to do a good job.

Her grandmother had taught her that.

Chapter Twenty-Five

Another surprise greeted LizBeth when she parked her car on the street in front of her apartment building. Not far off was Jackson's vehicle. And sitting on her stoop was Jackson himself. His elbows were resting on his thighs and his head was bent down, as if he were stretching his neck. Or exhausted.

Even though she couldn't see his face, she thought he looked worn out and tired.

"Jackson?" she called out as she approached. "Is everything all right?"

His head popped up. Then he quickly got to his feet. "Hey, LizBeth. How are you?"

"I'm good. I just got home from working all day at the store. How long have you been here?"

"A while." He glanced at his phone, which was clutched in his hand. "Maybe an hour?"

"An hour?" She walked to his side. "Why didn't you simply come over to Busy's? We could have talked, then."

"I didn't want to bother you there."

Her smile faltered as she realized Jackson wasn't

being completely honest. He looked worried, too. She wondered if all the worry was for his sister—or for something else. "It wouldn't have been a bother. But you know that, right?"

He rolled his neck. "Of course. Never mind. I... I think I'm just tired. Now, come here a little closer."

She took his outstretched hand but was anxious to make him smile. "Why do you need me to do that?"

"Why do you think?" he murmured as he tugged on her hand and brought her close enough for her to rest her palm on his chest. "I can't kiss you otherwise."

Surprised, LizBeth lifted her chin and accepted his sweet kiss. It was really little more than a brief brush of his lips against hers. But it was more than enough to encourage her to lean closer and snake her arms around his waist. After kissing him again, she hugged him before pulling out her keys. "Now, let's get you inside and cooled off."

"I'm all right."

"Maybe so, but I'll still fetch you something to drink. It's warm out here. I bet you're parched."

Jackson followed her inside and then to her small galley kitchen. "Don't go to any trouble for me, Liz-Beth. You worked all day."

"The day I think getting you a glass of lemonade is trouble is going to be a sad one," she said as she pulled down a pair of glasses and started filling them with ice. "Go have a seat. I'm going to get us a drink and then go freshen up a moment. I feel like I've got half the store's dust on me."

"No rush."

She smiled back at him but knew she'd hurry, anyway. There was something going on behind Jackson's eyes and she had no idea what it was. If he hadn't been so eager to kiss her hello, she might have worried about his feelings for her, but the two of them seemed solid.

After washing up in the bathroom and then slipping on a pair of old jeans and a T-shirt, she met him back in her living room.

Jackson was standing in front of one of her bookshelves and holding a small framed photo of her and a girlfriend at the Ohio State Fair. When he saw her approach, he placed it back on the shelf. "Sorry," he said. "I couldn't resist."

"That's Ellen and me at the state fair."

"You look happy."

"We were. Ellen grew up near downtown Cleveland. She'd never been around goats and sheep." Giggling at the memory, LizBeth added, "She was half enthralled and half grossed out by all the sights and smells in the livestock arena."

"I bet. Every once in a while, one of my police buddies will act as if chicken doesn't come from a farm but instead from the grocery store, neatly wrapped in plastic."

"Right?" Glad that he seemed to be relaxing a bit, she said, "So how does this place compare to yours? Is it a lot more cluttered? Or do you have a lot of things scattered around like me?" She didn't really care; all she wanted to do was talk about anything so his expression would ease.

As if he knew what she was attempting to do, Jackson made a show of looking around the room. "I wouldn't say this room is cluttered…but my place is definitely more sparse."

Attempting to see her small living room through his

eyes, she smiled. She not only had a small couch and two comfortable chairs, but a coffee table, two side tables, a television and a bookshelf crammed with books, photos and trinkets. Over the arm of one chair was a lovely quilt her mother had made for her twelfth birthday. There was also a basket of yarn, a pile of magazines and a metal watering can in the shape of a goat.

When he walked over to the goat and chuckled, she teased him. "What? You don't have any metal goat watering cans?"

"I'm afraid not. I mean, not yet, anyhow. However, if I was going to get one, I'd get one just like it."

She giggled. "Ellen gave it to me after our visit to the fair. She said that way I could always have a goat nearby."

"She sounds like a good friend."

"She is. The best." Taking a seat, she sipped her drink and propped her feet up on the table. "So is your sparse decorating style by choice or need?"

"A little of both, I guess." He paused a moment. "I used to wonder if it was because I didn't want to spend any money—or because I wasn't used to needing material things. But now I think it has more to do with the fact that I don't know what to get. I think a mule might have better decorating sense than I do."

"I'll be glad to help you, if you'd like." When he looked taken aback, she said, "I won't even make you put out quilts or goats."

A bit of the light that had been shining faded again. "I might take you up on it." Sipping his lemonade, he looked away.

"Hey, Jackson, why are you here?"

"I need to ask you some questions, LizBeth. And

yeah, I'm procrastinating because I don't know what you're going to say."

"It sounds serious."

"It is."

When he still waited, she asked, "Is this about your sister or your Jane Doe?"

"Both. I'm pretty certain they're connected."

"Okay. Well, we might as well get it over with, though I don't know how I can help. I already gave you the list of the Daisy Bag owners. I also gave you Mary's name."

"I know, and I appreciate that."

"Did you ever find out anything about her?"

"We looked and a sheriff I know asked around, but everyone seems to think she simply moved to another Amish community in Michigan."

"And?"

"And you know as well as I do that looking for an Old Order Amish woman in Michigan is about the same as searching for a needle in a haystack. No Amish woman is going to be listed anywhere, and even if she was, there's likely four dozen women by the same name."

LizBeth sighed. He was right. There were only about a dozen Amish last names, and though many people gave their children a variety of first names, the majority pulled names from the Bible. Mary was an extremely popular first name among the Amish.

"What about the bag? Was that a dead end, too?"

"It turns out the bag just happened to be with the woman we found. So while it did end up leading me to Aaron Zook, which I'm grateful for, we don't think every victim had a Daisy Bag with her."

"Every victim? Do you think there was more than one?"

Looking even more troubled, Jackson nodded. "It's looking that way, I'm afraid."

She turned to face him again. Was this his way of telling her goodbye? "Jackson, I'm starting to get confused. Are you trying to tell me that you need to head back to Cincinnati now?"

Like, for good?

"I will eventually, but I have some more work to do here first." He sighed. "LizBeth, there's no easy way to tell you this. I'm going to need to interview you about your employees."

"My employees?" She laughed softly. "Ah, I think you know I only have three. Ana from time to time, then Fern and Beth." Her eyes widened. "And sometimes Harlan, of course."

"Harlan is your cousin, right?"

"Right." Thinking quickly, she added, "To be honest, I wouldn't exactly call him an employee. He only works at Busy's a few hours a month. Maybe about eight? He only fills in when someone is sick or at Christmastime."

"All right. We won't worry about him, then. We'll concentrate on the others."

Jackson sounded so official she was starting to get nervous. "What do you want to know about Fern, Ana and Beth?"

He pulled out both his phone and a small notebook and pen from his jacket pockets. "I'm going to take notes, but do you mind if I record your answers as well?"

She started to smile, then realized he wasn't joking at all. Jackson was being completely serious. "You came over to question me about the case."

"Technically, yes."

"Is there any other reason?" When he hesitated, she realized she already had her answer. He wouldn't have come over just to see her.

He shifted uncomfortably. "I know I'm not making you very happy right now, but it can't be helped. This is important."

"Of course." Eager to get whatever he came for over with and then get him out of the house, she waved her hand. "Ask me whatever you need to."

"Thank you. And may I record our conversation?"

The way he was focusing on his proper protocols was beginning to get very irritating. "Yes, Jackson. Record whatever you want."

Looking perturbed but resolute, he flipped open his notebook, set his phone to Record and picked up the pen that had been resting on his lap. "Tell me about your employees, LizBeth."

"Like I said, I have four. My cousin Harlan, who is young and only fills in occasionally. Then there's Ana. She is young as well, and only works about ten to twelve hours a month."

"So your main employees are Beth and Fern."

"Yes." Feeling like she was repeating herself, Liz-Beth said, "What do you want to know?"

"Let's start with Beth. How many hours a week does she work for you?"

"Fifteen to twenty."

"Tell me a little bit about her. You know, her age and such."

"Beth is seventeen and a sweet girl. She's Amish and

likes to chat with everyone." She tried to think of something more but couldn't really think of anything to add.

"Have you known her long?"

"About two years, I guess. She came into the store soon after she turned sixteen and asked if I needed any more help. It had been a busy moment. So busy that I hired her on the spot!"

"Do you know much about her family?"

"Not really." When Jackson waited, obviously wanting more information, LizBeth added, "I've met her parents, of course, but I can't think of anything else to tell you about them or Beth. She's just a regular teenager."

"That's fine. Now tell me about Fern."

"Well, let's see. Fern works about twenty to twenty-five hours a week. She's worked at Busy's a long time, too. Longer than me."

His eyes narrowed. "How long, do you think?"

Jackson's pointed questions were starting to make her uncomfortable. She was getting the feeling that he wanted to learn something specific but she had no idea what he was hoping to hear. "I don't know how long Fern's worked at the store. Maybe twelve years?"

"What does she usually do when she's working?"

LizBeth shrugged. "Fern does the same sort of things that Beth and I do. She helps customers, straightens the store, works at the cash register, unpacks new merchandise…" Her voice drifted off. "I don't know what else to say, Jackson. Fern is just, well, Fern." LizBeth smiled. "If you knew her well, you'd understand what I mean."

Jackson's expression didn't lighten a bit. "How does Fern get along with the customers?"

"Fine, I guess." It occurred to her then that she'd never actually given much thought to that. Fern had been such a fixture in the store for so long LizBeth had taken her for granted.

But instead of relaxing and leaning back, Jackson's expression turned even more intense. "You guess? What does that mean?"

"Jackson, what is wrong?" she asked impatiently. "Why are you asking so many questions about my employees? They're just two Amish women. That's it."

"Please, just answer the question. Does she speak to all the customers? Only Amish ones? Are there some people she talks to more often than others?"

Sally's comments about Fern being a good gossip came to mind. So did the way the woman had looked at Fern, almost warily. But if she relayed that comment to Jackson, was that wrong? "I've, ah, recently heard someone say that Fern liked to gossip and was sometimes a little judgmental, but I don't know if that is important or not."

He lifted his pencil. "How was she judgmental? What did she say or do?"

"I... I'm not really sure. I only heard that she was."

"You've never witnessed this?"

"No."

"Are you sure?"

He was making her nervous. "Yes. I mean, I don't know. I think I'm sure."

"Think, LizBeth. Have you ever witnessed Fern getting upset with a customer for not acting like they should?"

"Maybe." Seen through a different lens, maybe Fern

had been too judgmental, but how could she be sure she was remembering every interaction correctly?

"I need something more specific from you."

His tone was clipped and his attitude was bordering on belligerent. She didn't care for it one bit. "Maybe I need more information, Jackson. What is this all about, anyway? You're acting like Fern had something to do with your Amish Jane Doe!" When he just stared at her, she felt her mouth go dry. "Oh, my word. That's exactly what you're saying, isn't it?"

"Are you saying that you can't think of any specific instances when Fern might have been upset or found fault with a customer?"

Another instance flashed in her mind, when two girls, both obviously in the middle of their *rumspringa*, had come in the store with two boys. One of them had been wearing lipstick—or at least still had stained lips from it. Fern had gotten so angry about it that LizBeth had had to tell her to calm down.

She considered sharing that, but it was silly. And with the mood Jackson was in, he'd probably go find those girls and interview them.

So instead LizBeth simply nodded. "Yes, that's what I'm saying."

He pressed his phone again, ending the recording. With a sigh, he said, "LizBeth, I need to let you know that it's a crime to withhold information or evidence in a criminal investigation. If you are keeping something from me, I'll be really disappointed."

She stood up. "I'm not. Now, will you finally tell me what is going on?"

"I'm sorry, I can't." Jackson stood up as well, sliding his phone and notepad back into a jacket pocket. "Thank you for the lemonade."

When he headed toward her front door, she hurried after him. "Wait. You can't just leave. I need to know what this was all about. I mean, you're making me think Fern is somehow involved with your cold case."

When Jackson just stared at her, she felt a chill all the way to her toes. "You really think so? You must be wrong. Fern might be a stickler for rules, but she wouldn't harm a fly."

"Don't say anything to anyone about this investigation, LizBeth."

"Who would I say anything to?" Honestly, she was getting pretty irritated with him. She knew he was a cop, but he was practically acting like they were strangers instead of close friends.

"I mean it. I'm serious."

"Believe me, I understand you're serious about this case." He *was* serious about his case. About her? Maybe not, after all. She opened the door. "God speed, Jackson. And goodbye."

After giving her another long look, he walked out the door.

Leaving her to wonder what in the world had just happened.

Chapter Twenty-Six

Jackson knew he'd injured LizBeth's feelings. He knew he could've been kinder and more understanding about her answers—and not fired off so many questions like they were in the middle of an interrogation. However, he'd known he had no choice but to be cool and matter of fact. He recorded the conversation for accountability and to share with his superiors. He couldn't give anyone a reason to discount LizBeth's answers. Experience told him that he was going to need all the ammunition he could in order to press charges against Fern if she didn't confess.

But as he started his vehicle and dwelled on the last look she'd given him, he wondered if he might have done the right thing for the investigation but the wrong thing for this relationship with LizBeth. Doubts filled him. Had he once again placed a personal relationship behind professional duty?

When his phone's ringer interrupted his thoughts, he reached for it with a feeling of relief.

"Lapp."

"Jackson Lapp, hiya. This here is Mose. I heard you've been trying to pin me down."

Mose Kramer was an experienced sheriff, most recently coming out of Kentucky. He was glad this was the man he had to work with, given that Mose had a reputation for getting things done and treating everyone in his jurisdiction—whether they were Amish, English or Mennonite—with respect but also with a firm hand.

"I have," he said at last. "I mean, thanks for calling me back."

"What can I help you with?"

Briefly, Jackson relayed the news about his sister's abduction, Aaron Zook's arrest and finally his bombshell about Fern's involvement. To his relief, Mose seemed inclined to listen to him without interrupting.

When he finished at last, Jackson added, "I'm hoping you'll go with me to Fern's house, Mose."

"I'll be glad to, but I have to tell ya, this is sounding like it's coming out of left field."

Though Jackson had a feeling that Fern was absolutely involved with his case in some way, he also knew how Mose felt. It was hard not to feel protective of one's town's citizens. Especially someone like Fern, who was a longtime resident and had never caused trouble.

"You might be right," Jackson said in an easy tone. "But if Aaron's statement can be trusted, a young woman's death might finally be put to bed."

"Her death—and her parents' misery. There's nothing worse than not knowing what has happened to a child. That's a special sort of pain, I reckon."

"Do you want to meet me at Fern's?" He passed on

the address, having gotten it from the state's tax records.

"*Jah*, I can be there in ten."

"I'll see you there."

When Jackson pulled up in front of Fern Hershberger's neat-as-a-pin home, Mose was already there. He'd parked a few houses down and was leaning against his cruiser, typing something on his phone. He walked over to meet Jackson when he got out.

"Ready?"

Jackson nodded, but he didn't move.

"What's wrong? You're not having second thoughts, are you?"

"No. This feels right. Aaron's story felt right and Fern's involvement connected a lot of dots." After debating for a moment, he added, "I guess there's a part of me that hates this is how I've returned to Berlin. Twelve years ago, I left after causing trouble at a party and was later shunned. Now, when I've finally returned for a visit, all I've done is raise a lot of questions. Worse, I'm about to arrest a supposedly beloved member of the community."

"I think you're misrepresenting things a bit. You returned because of a murder, not to sightsee. Let's also not forget that your sister was abducted! You ain't the only person causing trouble around here."

"Everything you're saying is true." Jackson wanted to add more but shrugged instead. How could he explain that he felt almost guilty for everything that had happened?

Mose studied him for a moment. "You've obviously been out of Holmes County too long, young man."

"And you say this because?"

"Because you've forgotten a tried and true rule around here. And that is no one group is free of faults. Not Amish boys who jump the fence. Not pesky tourists from Canada or Texas. Not progressive Mennonites or Catholics or…" he paused "…someone who is Old Order Amish. Everyone walks through their life as best they can. It ain't your fault if one old lady with an evil heart might be a murderer." He shook his finger. "But it would be your fault if you let yourself worry about things you have no control over. Ain't so?"

"Right," Jackson said. "Thanks."

Mose slapped him on the back. "Let's go have a chat. Who knows? You might be barking up the wrong tree, after all."

"I hope not, but you're right." Feeling better and more at ease, he led the way to Fern's door and knocked.

She answered after less than a minute. "Yes?"

"Miss Hershberger, my name is Jackson Lapp and this is—"

"Mose Kramer," she finished as she eyed Mose in a cool manner. "I know Mose."

"Ma'am," Mose said politely.

Fern rolled her eyes. "What do you two want?"

"We came to ask you some questions," Jackson said.

"About what?" She still didn't move from the doorway.

"May we come in? This might take a while."

"Is this necessary?" Looking at Mose, she asked, "What if I say *nee*?"

"That is your right, Fern," Mose said easily. "I'll just escort you down to the police station and we can visit there."

"You canna do that."

"I surely can. Now, which would you prefer?"

Fern's eyes darted between Jackson and Mose... and then seemed to catch sight of a neighbor across the street. "People are looking. They're going to know that the sheriff came here. And you, too, Jackson Lapp," she added, her expression accusing. "I won't be able to face them for weeks."

Jackson was about out of patience. "Which would you prefer, ma'am? I'm not going to wait more than ten more seconds."

Fern glanced his way. Whatever she saw in his eyes must have given her pause, because she backed up and held the door open farther. "Fine. Come in. But watch your shoes."

They entered the room, immediately feeling the temperature drop a good ten degrees in the dark house. Just as he closed the door behind him, he heard Fern say to Mose, "Wait. You canna just go in—"

Seconds later, Mose was opening a shade and calling out for him. "Jackson, come in here. You've gotta see this."

Struck by the other man's grim tone, Jackson entered a small room just off the kitchen—and felt like he was entering the twilight zone. Not only was there a working light plugged into the wall, but there were photographs all over the walls. Photos of young women with black *x*'s slashed over them.

Including, if he weren't mistaken, one blue-eyed, blond Amish girl with freckles across her nose.

There was no doubt about it. There, in living color, was the woman who had haunted his dreams. His Amish Jane Doe.

Chapter Twenty-Seven

While Mose pulled out his phone, first to call for backup, then to take pictures of Fern's walls, Jackson went to see Fern. She was standing next to the front door with a militant expression on her face and her arms crossed on her chest.

"I saw the photos, Fern."

She didn't so much as blink. "I'm assuming that means you have questions for me."

"I do. Want to tell me why you have those women's pictures on your wall?"

She raised her chin. "It's obvious, don't you think?"

"Not to me. Besides, I'd rather hear what you have to say."

"I doubt you're gonna want to hear what I have to say about your sister."

Fern's voice had turned almost gleeful. Jackson realized then that she didn't have a single bit of remorse for her actions. Instead, she seemed proud.

Never had Jackson wished more that he wasn't required by an oath he'd taken to listen to what she had to say and not respond. "You're wrong. I do want to hear everything you think about both my sister and the other women whose pictures are on your wall."

"You sure? It all ain't good."

"All good isn't the truth, though, is it?"

"You believe that?"

"Of course." He pretended to do some thinking. "You know, I bet the two of us aren't that different."

"How so?"

"I became a police officer to make sure people followed the rules. Following the rules and obeying laws is important to me. I have a feeling that's important to you, too."

"It is. It's important to our way of life and it's important to the Lord."

He folded his arms over his chest, mimicking her posture. "You know, I've noticed that some people in the Amish community don't take the *Ordnung* as seriously as they ought."

"No one does. Some of the young girls and boys don't even want to work much anymore." She pursed her lips. "Not like back in my day. Not like I still work now."

"What do you think they need?"

"Consequences," she said immediately. "Consequences so severe that they'll think twice about doing something wrong."

And Fern just happened to have elected herself the arresting officer, judge and jury. With effort, Jackson asked, "What do you think should happen?"

"What should happen is that young'uns' parents get involved. That the preachers and the bishop need to tell them what's what." She glared. "But that isn't how it always goes, is it?"

Playing along, Jackson shook his head. "You're right. Not everyone wants to do the hard things."

Her eyes gleamed. "You're exactly right. It ain't easy to take a stand for the greater good. But someone has to."

"Are those photographs of the women you made sure learned the rules? Who you made sure learned right from wrong?"

"*Jah.*" She blinked, looked confused for a moment, then blurted, "And *jah*, I do know that I'm not supposed to be taking pictures of anyone. That we're supposed to believe that's bad, but I had my reasons, Jackson Lapp. I needed to do it."

"Why is that?" he asked, aware that Mose had come out of the room and was listening to Fern's words intently.

"So I would have proof. Proof that they needed to be taught a lesson."

"What happened to the girls after you asked Aaron to escort them out of town?"

"You know he was working with me, then?"

He noticed that she didn't look upset. Instead, she seemed even more proud of herself. "I guessed, and then he told me that you sometimes chose the girls he would drive."

As he'd hoped, she looked offended. "There weren't no *sometimes* at all. *I* was the one who did all the choosing. Not him. I was in charge, not him." She nodded again. "Aaron only did what I wanted him to."

"Well, after he did your bidding, what happened?"

"Oh, well, I found me a man in downtown Cincinnati who was always looking for young girls for some of his customers."

"Customers? What kind of customers?"

"What kind do you think?" Her voice was thick with derision. "The kind of customers who would want loose women like those girls. They learned not to be so brazen, I tell you that."

"How do you know?"

For the first time since they'd started their conversation, Fern looked confused. "How do I know what?"

"How do you know they learned their lesson? Did you bring them back?"

"Of course not." She looked horrified. "Those girls would have tainted the rest of us."

"What did happen to them, then?"

Fern looked away. "I don't know."

"Really? You just left them there?"

"I got them out of here. That's all that matters."

He pulled out the picture of the girl who had haunted him for weeks. "Who is this?"

"That? That's Elizabeth."

"Elizabeth who?"

"Schrock."

"Is she one of the brazen girls you had to make sure left the county?"

Fern wrinkled her nose. "To be sure."

"So what did she do?"

"Sorry?"

Unable to help himself, he hardened his voice. "Fern, what did Elizabeth Schrock do that was so terrible?"

She blinked. Looked almost confused. "I… I told you, she was brazen. She was bad."

"You already said that. Give me a specific example."

She looked bewildered again. Almost lost. "It was a long time ago. I don't remember exactly."

That was all he needed to know to go ahead and make his arrest.

"Fern Hershberger, Elizabeth Schrock is the reason I came back to Berlin. Her body was found two years ago. She'd been murdered after being raped. There were needle marks on her arms and evidence of being bound and abused. She was buried without a funeral and without any prayers for her soul. Her parents still have no idea what happened to her. For two years, her case sat in a file, forgotten. That is the consequence of your actions."

She shook her head. "*Nee*. I didn't do any of that."

Mose stepped forward. "No, Fern, you just made sure it happened." He took out a pair of restraints. "Fern Hershberger, you are under arrest for aiding and abetting kidnapping, withholding evidence, human trafficking and for your part in the murder of Elizabeth Schrock. May God have mercy on your soul."

She shook her head. "*Nee*."

"Will you come willingly with me or should I restrain you?"

"*Nee*, I ain't going anywhere. This is my home. I am a good woman. A pure one."

Jackson was unable to help himself any longer. "You are a great many things, but pure isn't one of them."

After he read Fern her rights, Mose reached for her elbow. "Come with me, Fern."

She walked beside him with her head down, never asking for her purse or even to lock her house.

While Mose got her situated in his cruiser, Jackson

located Fern's simple black purse, pulled out the set of keys in a side pocket and locked the door.

Soon, he would have to return with a team. They'd spend several hours combing through the house, searching for more information about the women Fern targeted. They'd also comb the area for anything that could help cement the case against her.

So there was still a lot to be done.

But not yet. Right now, all he wanted to do was get out of the house. Leave this place, Fern's world and everything she had put into motion behind. At least for a while.

More than anything, Jackson wanted to feel clean again.

Chapter Twenty-Eight

The early morning sunrise had been beautiful. The sun had risen over the fields, bringing with it a band of gold that made everything in its rays look shiny and new.

It looked as if the day was going to be just as lovely. Low humidity, warm and blue skies with not a cloud in sight. After the recent events, LizBeth found herself taking note of every single beautiful gift the Lord had brought. Though she felt a bit uneasy given the many surprises she'd encountered of late, she did feel especially grateful for every gift the Lord had brought. If she'd learned anything, it was that it was wrong to take anything for granted. One never knew when something might get taken away.

All of this was why she was trying to keep an open mind about being at work so early in the morning. LizBeth couldn't remember the last time she'd been at the store at seven o'clock. Fern had always volunteered to meet any early deliveries, and LizBeth had been so grateful for that.

Now, as she walked around the empty store, filled

with memories from both her grandmother and so many years working behind the counter, LizBeth realized she felt almost as empty inside as the aisles of the market were. No, maybe even more so, since she felt barren inside.

She'd never thought there was a difference between the two words, but she certainly thought so now. *Empty* was simply lacking or missing something. *Barren*, on the other hand, felt more negative, as in she wasn't just feeling a huge gap in her life, but she felt almost dead inside. Without hope.

The door's bells jangled as Jackson entered. He was wearing faded jeans, boots, a knit collared shirt and a light tan blazer. He looked handsome and professional. She realized now that if she hugged him, she would likely feel the holster on his side.

He also looked so far from the hurting, vulnerable young man she'd fallen in love with. It was hard to realize this grown man was the same teenage boy who used to pass her notes in school.

He was right on time.

"Hey," she said as she walked out of the shadows. "You're as punctual as ever."

"Am I? Well, that's something I guess." He held up a brown paper sack that she hadn't even realized he was holding. "I brought sustenance. Where do you want to sit?"

The break room would bring back too many memories of visiting with Fern. "Would you like to eat outside? The weather's nice and there's a small picnic table just behind the store," she said as she locked the door so no customers would decide to wander in at such an early hour.

"Sorry, but could we eat inside instead? I'd rather not take off this blazer in public since I've got on a holster. The sun is already warm."

LizBeth was disappointed but couldn't fault his reasons. Besides, she was going to have to get used to spending time in the break room sooner or later. "That's fine. There's a room back here we can use." She led the way down the hall.

Jackson followed. He didn't say a word but she could almost sense that he had a lot on his mind—and intended to say it all. LizBeth could practically feel his gaze drilling into her back.

The moment they got inside, she turned on a small lamp on a side table. It cast a dim glow throughout the space.

"You have electricity in here."

After clearing off a few wholesale catalogs, she sat down at the small rickety metal table. "Yeah. About a year after I took over the shop, I added an electrical line in to power the commercial refrigerators and freezers. I know Busy never had a problem using gas lines but a few months after I took over, there was a gas leak and it kind of freaked me out. I decided to add the line for peace of mind." She shrugged. "Plus, I'm not Amish, so I didn't feel too guilty about it."

"I wasn't judging. I was just surprised." He pulled out two paper cups and an insulated thermos, pouring a cup of coffee for each of them.

She supposed she did sound a little defensive. "Sorry, I guess I'm feeling a little off today."

He exhaled as he pulled out a couple of pastries, each wrapped in waxed paper. "It's not the healthiest snack, but I love these crullers."

"I do, too." She smiled as she took an exploratory sip from her cup. "Jackson, this coffee is really good."

"Thanks." He looked pleased.

After taking another sip, she said, "I can't believe you carry a stainless thermos with you."

"It's the nature of the job, I guess," he replied as he took a sip from his own cup. "I've learned to do things that make being in a car for five or six hours at a time more bearable."

"Does this thermos mean you're about to be back in the car for several hours?"

He winced. "I'm afraid so. I arrested Fern last night, LizBeth. She spent the night in a cell over at the sheriff's office. I'll be taking her to Cincinnati this morning."

Though she'd known this was going to happen, it was still hard to believe that Fern had been so instrumental in the death of his Jane Doe. "You're really positive she's responsible for your Jane Doe?"

He nodded. "I can't share very much, but we discovered a lot of incriminating evidence in her house that Fern didn't deny. I'm afraid she's responsible for more than one woman going missing from the area."

Tears filled her eyes. "I can't believe it."

"I think we were all taken by surprise. Even though I'm well aware that no Amish person is without faults, Fern's actions and motivations were shocking."

She wiped her eyes. She still didn't want to believe Jackson's words, but she was beginning to realize that he was shaken, too. "I see."

"LizBeth, look… I really am sorry to have to tell you this news, especially when you two were so close.

I know this must be hard on you. I wish the case had turned out differently."

"I wish it had, too." She sipped from her cup again, then forced herself to stop dwelling on her feelings. "Do you think Fern had something to do with Marie's abduction, too?"

Jackson shrugged. "I can't say for certain but it's likely."

She took a small bite of the cruller donut but could barely swallow the treat. It was too sweet, too much for her nerves, it seemed.

After the uncomfortable silence dragged on for another thirty seconds, she cleared her throat and finally broached what had been heavy on her mind. "Where does that leave us?"

"To tell you the truth, I'm not sure."

That answer was almost harder to hear than Fern's involvement. "I see."

He shook his head. "No, I don't think you do. Liz-Beth, I still care for you. A lot. I still want to have a relationship with you, too. I just… I need to know how you're feeling."

"I feel the same way about you, Jackson. However, it's going to be hard to have the close, real relationship that I've always wanted."

"Do you really think so?"

"We're going to be living in two different parts of the state. An almost three-hour drive from door to door can't be ignored."

"I know it might be challenging, but we could make it work. Don't you think?"

She shrugged. "I think we could try, but for how long? I mean, eventually either you are going to have to come here or I'm going to have to move south to Cincinnati, right?"

He nodded slowly as he reached for her hand. "Look, I still need to go see my parents and Marie before I collect Fern and head down to Cincy."

"I understand."

Jackson looked even more torn. "LizBeth, I'd love nothing more than to push everything and everyone else to the side for a few days so you and I can figure things out. But I can't."

"Of course you can't. I'd be surprised if you did."

"Maybe we can at least agree to talk about this some more on the phone?"

"We could, I guess." Even though it felt like they were delaying the inevitable, she wasn't eager to simply tell him goodbye for good. Jackson had once again snuck into her life before she could think about the consequences to her heart. Now that she knew just how painful being without him was going to be, LizBeth was willing to wait a bit. At least until she felt she had no other choice.

He squeezed her hand before releasing it. "Thanks."

She smiled at him as he stood up. "Be careful, Jackson."

"You, too," he said. He looked like he was about to add something more, but his phone dinged and he turned away. With the briefest of waves, he walked out of the break room. Seconds later, she heard the faint click of a dead bolt followed by bells jangling.

He was gone again.

"He's here, Marie," her mother said excitedly from her position by the living room window. "Why don't you go let your *bruder* in?"

Marie rolled her eyes as she headed to the door. That comment was so typical of her parents. After years of refusing to say Jackson's name, now he was back in the fold, just like he'd never left in the first place. Of course, it hadn't occurred to them to explain themselves to her, either. As with everything else, she was just supposed to accept their choice and do whatever they wanted.

She didn't care about things like that anymore, though. Now she had Jackson back in her life—and a taste of what her life could have been like if she hadn't escaped from Aaron at the gas station. There was bad... and then there was very, very bad.

"Jackson," she said with a smile. "I'm so happy to see you."

"Come here, Marie," he said gently. "I almost lost you yesterday. I'm going to need a hug."

She threw herself into his arms and he held her close. And then, even though she hadn't thought she had any tears left, she started crying again. Big noisy tears complete with hiccups. "Sorry," she gasped as she attempted to pull away. "I don't know what's gotten into me."

"I do." Keeping his hands on her upper arms, he pulled back a bit so she could see his own tear-streaked face. "You're feeling as grateful as I am. Ain't so?"

She nodded. "I'm so glad you're here."

Some of his smile faded. "I am, too, sister. May I come in?"

"*Jah*, sure." After she closed the door behind him, she whispered. "Be prepared, *Mamm* and *Daed* are both eager to see ya."

"I am eager to see them, too. Almost as eager as I

was to see you." He rested his hand on the middle of her back. "Let's go sit for a spell. Together, we'll see what they have to say."

They might not really know each other anymore. And Marie knew they likely had a lot of questions to ask each other. But there was still something so familiar about being next to him. And yes, letting him take the lead with their parents. His presence calmed her. It always had.

Mamm and *Daed* were sitting side by side on the couch in the living room, as if they hadn't been eagerly awaiting his arrival.

For once, neither was reading, whittling, knitting or doing any other type of project. When they caught sight of Jackson, they looked visibly relieved.

"Jackson, you came back," *Daed* said.

"Of course. I couldn't leave Berlin without stopping by here first."

Some of the optimism Marie had been feeling faded. "You're leaving already?" she asked before she could stop herself. "But you just got here."

"I know, but I have some things I have to work on—including making sure the case against Aaron Zook is solid."

"But then you'll come back?" *Mamm* asked.

"I will, but it might be a few days." Looking even more uncomfortable, he added, "Maybe even a couple of weeks."

But what about me? Marie wanted to scream. Instead, she sat down on an uncomfortable wooden chair and folded her hands on her lap.

"We are grateful that you helped Marie," *Daed* said. "I know I haven't been there for her, but I would like to be now." As if he could feel her pain, Jackson turned to face her. "Marie, I am *not* abandoning you. I want to be a part of your life from now on."

Not trusting her voice, she nodded but said nothing.

"I'm sure Marie will be grateful for your attention," their father said piously.

"Indeed," said *Mamm*. "We will all look forward to your visits when you get back this way."

Suddenly, all Marie could envision was a lifetime of being stuck back in the house and having to ask her parents' permission to do even the smallest of activities. No doubt, she would grow so tired of their interference that she would one day agree to marry the person of their choosing—just so she could get away.

She'd be stuck in the same place, just in a different situation. She couldn't do it. She simply could not.

As every worry churned inside her, she knew she couldn't be the dutiful daughter any more. "*Nee!*" she burst out. "No, this isn't okay."

Her mother's eyebrows nearly hit her hairline. "Marie, calm yourself."

She got to her feet. "*Nee*, I won't! I was abducted yesterday. *Yesterday*. It was awful. Aaron hurt me. He scared me. I thought... I thought I would never see any of you again."

"You would have," Jackson said. "I would have found you no matter what."

"I'm sure you would've, but I was the one who escaped. I'm the one who got out and screamed for help." Looking at each of her family members, she added, "I know I'm only eighteen, but I'm strong, too. I don't want to be afraid any longer."

Their father nodded. "You will be safe here. I'll make sure of it."

"You don't understand. I love you both but I don't want to always fear that I'll get in trouble. And I don't want to worry that I'll never see you again, Jackson."

Jackson looked at her intently. "Marie, what do you want? Are you trying to say that you want to jump the fence?"

"I thought I might, but now I know that I don't. I like being Amish. I like our community. But I do want more freedom."

"Marie, we are trying to protect you," *Mamm* said.

"Isn't there a way I can be protected without you two being so difficult?" To her dismay, Jackson grinned. "This isn't funny, Jackson!"

He stood up and knelt in front of her. "Of course it isn't. It's just that I wish I had been half as brave as you are now, little sister. *Mamm*, *Daed*, I'll be back. Please don't lose her." After kissing her on the head, he stood in front of his parents. "I know we have a long road until things are better, but I'd like to try."

"I'd like that, too," *Mamm* said.

His father simply stood up and hugged him. "I never thought God would be so good as to let us see you again. I want to try, too."

"I'm sorry, but I've got to go. I have to transport someone down to Cincinnati."

"Be safe."

"*Danke*. I will." Turning to Marie, he said, "I'm going to call you every day. You call me back whenever you want."

"And you'll answer?"

"I will if it's at all possible. If I don't, it will only be because I'm working. I promise."

Marie turned to their parents. "Do you two promise that I can speak to Jackson whenever I want?"

"*Jah*, child," her mother murmured.

At last, Marie nodded. "All right, then."

Jackson placed his hands on her shoulders. "Marie, I am not leaving you for good. I'll be back here soon. I promise."

He turned and walked out before anyone could say another word.

When it was just the three of them again, the silence felt as harsh and strained as it ever had. "I'll go work in the garden," she mumbled.

"Hold on, daughter," her father said.

Here it came. He was going to punish her for being mouthy and for losing her temper. Now that he knew Jackson wasn't going to come right back, their father wasn't going to worry about him getting upset.

She stood in front of him. "Yes?"

"What is it you want to do?"

"I don't just want to talk to Jackson, I want to do other things, too. I want to be able to go to Busy's market on my own. Or have lunch with a girlfriend. Or go to the park with my friends."

After looking at her mother, *Daed* nodded. "All right."

"All right?" That was it?

"You are not the only person who feels like it's time for some changes, Marie. I don't want to drive you away. I already drove away one child, and I don't want to do that to two."

"Next time you want to go have your lunch with a

girlfriend, all you have to do is let us know," *Mamm* whispered. "We will give you permission."

Marie wanted to believe them, but she wasn't going to hold her breath, either. But maybe they would surprise her. There was always that chance. The Lord had already proven that anything was possible. "*Danke.* Um, I will go garden now."

When they didn't respond, she walked out the door. Maybe Jackson was right. Maybe things were changing for the better, after all.

Chapter Twenty-Nine

After everything that had happened, Jackson felt that transporting Fern back to Cincinnati and then interrogating her about Elizabeth seemed almost anticlimactic. Ever since Fern's horrific misdeeds had been discovered, most of the wind had left the proud woman's sails. Fern no longer acted belligerent or defiant. Instead, she was docile and quiet—almost like a shell of her former self.

One of the newest officers at CPD had even mentioned that Fern looked like nothing more than an older Amish woman who had wandered into the police station by accident.

If Jackson hadn't seen the evidence in her home for himself, he would have almost felt sorry for her. But since he had, he felt nothing for Fern Hershberger but contempt.

After Sergeant Gunther and he completed the interrogation and they were able to match Fern's DNA with some of the items in Elizabeth's Daisy Bag, Jackson pressed formal charges for a variety of felonies. The judge agreed to keep her in jail until her trial date.

Some had thought that keeping Fern locked up was a bit too vigilant, but Jackson didn't trust her one bit. He felt she was upset about being caught, not sorry for what she had done.

A little over a week later, another arrest had been made—Fern's customer in the city, a Realtor no one would have looked at twice. Further investigation of this man led to his client list—and this time, thanks to DNA testing, Elizabeth's killer had been identified. Although her murderer had been recently responsible for another brutal killing, he wouldn't face trial. His drug-abused body had been found a day ago, lying facedown in his prison cell. He'd OD'd. It was a bittersweet end, but Jackson could close the case. He knew he should feel proud and triumphant.

Instead, all he felt was a sense of loss.

Days passed. As he'd promised, he checked in with Marie every day. He had meetings with other officers about Aaron and he completed reams of paperwork on Fern's case. Mose and he worked together on tracing the identity of the other women on Fern's wall.

And every night, after coming home and taking a much-needed shower, he called LizBeth.

Though she always answered and they often talked for an hour or more, Jackson couldn't help but feel that he was steadily losing ground with her. Maybe he didn't even blame LizBeth for being a little subdued. After all, time and again, he put his needs and his job in front of hers.

It was time to put her first and show her how much he cared, but he wasn't sure what to do. How could he do that without making her leave her grandmother's market?

Desperate for advice, he ended up calling Mose, of all people. Even though Mose was older, he'd only been married two years.

After relaying his and LizBeth's story over the phone, he said, "I know we're not exactly close friends, but I feel that I have a lot to learn from you. What do you think?"

"I think you've already made your decision, Jackson. I think what you're looking for is encouragement."

"No, that's not right. Don't you understand? I don't know what to do about me and LizBeth."

"So, out of all the people in your life, you've called me, *jah*?"

What was that supposed to mean? "That's true, but—"

"Jackson, I waited a real long time to get married. And though I know the Lord was just biding His time for me to find the right woman, I know He had something else in mind as well."

"What was it?"

"See, for years and years, I felt alone. I felt like I existed between two worlds."

Jackson struggled to understand. "As if you were living between your Amish past and your *Englisch* one?"

"*Nee*. I'm talking about my professional and personal lives. I didn't balance them. Jackson, it took a convoluted murder investigation back in Crittenden County to shake some sense into me. That case reminded me that life is precious."

"I get what you're saying now."

"Do you? Because if you do, then I'm sure you understand what I mean when I say that some things matter even more than solving crimes."

His mouth went dry. Mose was exactly right. Liz-Beth was more important to him than solving a crime. Marie was, too. He wanted both his sister and LizBeth to recognize that he loved them dearly.

But how could he do that without asking either one of them to leave everything they'd known so he could do his job?

"Mose, thank you for listening and for the advice. I appreciate it."

"But?"

"But... I don't know how to make everything work."

Mose made an impatient noise. "I think you do. You just don't want to see it."

"Mose, I didn't call you for Amish wisdom. I don't want to think about it some more. I need some answers. What do you think I should do?"

"Fine, son. How about this? Cincinnati ain't the only place in Ohio where there's cold cases. Stop being so narrow-minded and look around ya."

Jackson grinned. At last, he had his answer.

Chapter Thirty

A whole month had passed since LizBeth had stood in her shop with Jackson and realized it was going to be impossible for them to be together.

Since that moment, Jackson had called her almost every night. The calls had been good, too. They'd learned a lot about each other and filled in the gaps that the dozen years apart had left.

Jackson had been open and honest about his faults— and had seemed to do everything he could to make sure that she knew he truly cared about her.

Sometimes, when they'd tried to end their phone conversations late in the night, each of them had come very close to revealing their feelings. More than once, LizBeth had been tempted to tell Jackson that she still loved him. But each time she was about to say the words, self-preservation made her stop. If she declared her love for Jackson and he remained silent, she was sure she would feel even worse than she already did.

When she wasn't talking to Jackson at night and dealing with the fallout from Fern's terrible dealings, LizBeth spent a lot of time with Marie.

She'd been sure that Marie would be suffering after being abducted by Aaron—and by the realization of what had almost happened to her. However, if anything, the girl seemed more at peace than ever before.

Most of the anger in her soul had dissipated. Marie acted more sure of herself and smiled more. She also seemed to genuinely like hanging out at the store with LizBeth. To LizBeth's surprise, Marie's visits had even been encouraged by her parents.

Perhaps it really was never too late to change.

On Friday night, almost a month to the day from when she'd said goodbye to Jackson, LizBeth closed the shop by herself. It had been a quiet day at the store and the hours had dragged. All she wanted to do was go for a walk and order a pizza for dinner.

When the bells at the front of the store rang, she turned in annoyance. "Store's closed," she said before she caught sight of who had come in. "Jackson?"

"*Jah.* It's me." Looking pleased with himself, his hand hovered over the dead bolt. "Are you all alone? Can I lock the door?"

"I'm alone," she replied.

He clicked the dead bolt into place, then tossed the light jacket and backpack he'd been carrying on the floor. "I'm sorry it took me so long," he said.

She walked around the counter to get a better look at him. Today, he was wearing dark jeans, black boots… and a polo shirt with the Millersberg Police Department logo on it?

"What's going on? Why are you wearing that shirt?" she asked. "And what do you mean, sorry it took you so long? I didn't even know you were coming to town."

Jackson's gaze seemed to drift over her features as

eagerly as she'd taken in his. LizBeth stood still, letting him look his fill. It was the end of a ten-hour workday. She had on a long printed skirt, a V-neck blue T-shirt and navy flats. Her hair had long since been fastened into a ponytail.

"You look beautiful," he said.

As shocked as she was to see him, and confused about everything he'd been saying, she couldn't help but smile. "I look like a girl who's been working at her grandmother's store all day."

He drew closer. Reached for her hands. "You look like LizBeth. Like the girl I fell in love with so many years ago."

He'd said it! He'd said the words. "You love me."

"I love you," he repeated. "I'd love to say I never stopped, but I don't know if that's how it was. All I know is that life got in the way but now I'm back."

"Back with me? Back here?"

"Both." He took a deep breath. "LizBeth, I applied and got a job with the Millersberg PD. I quit the cold case unit in Cincinnati."

"Truly?"

"There's no way I was going to ask you to leave your grandmother's store."

"So you came to me." She gaped at him. "This… this is wonderful."

Jackson smiled again. "Well, it's okay." When she gaped at him again, he laughed. "It would be better if I knew you loved me, too."

That wasn't hard to share. "I love you, too."

"Truly?" he asked, repeating her word.

"Oh, yes."

Pulling her closer, he said, "One day, I'm hoping

maybe we can do all the things we used to talk about doing. You know…get married, have *kinner*, be happy."

Tears pricked her eyes. Those were the things they used to dream about back when they were still teenagers. All they'd ever wanted was to have simple things that mattered—not a lot of money, prestige or a big house. Just each other and a family to raise.

He leaned down and kissed her cheek. "What do you think, LizBeth? Could you do those things with me? One day?"

She nodded as she wrapped her arms around his neck. "Yes, Jackson Lapp. I can be happy with you, without a doubt. As far as I'm concerned, we've waited long enough."

He kissed her then, showing without words how much she meant to him. She kissed him back with all the longing in her heart. Yes, this perfect moment had been a long time coming, but some things were certainly worth the wait.

* * * * *